fighting for *her heart*

TARA GRACE ERICSON

LOVE ON SANCTUARY SHORES

Edited by Editing Done Write
Cover Design: Josh Bodden

Paperback ISBN-13: 978-1-949896-67-1
Ebook ISBN-13: 978-1-949896-68-8

"He has made everything beautiful in its time. He has also set eternity in the human heart; yet no one can fathom what God has done from beginning to end."

Ecclesiastes 3:11

one

CHLOE

THE EARLY MORNING SUNLIGHT ALL BUT SMACKED CHLOE in the face, glinting off the newest layer of snow as she stepped outside. The snow sparkled cheerfully in the sun, but by this time of the year, the white fluff had ceased feeling magical, and she was itching for spring. Her keys jingled as she turned to lock the door of her small cottage, breaking the otherwise silent morning.

Usually, she was up before the sun, but with no guests staying at the bed-and-breakfast, her services weren't required. Unfortunately, it was a common problem during the off-season. That was the way of life here on Sanctuary Island. In the late spring through early autumn, the island would be bustling with an influx of tourists, enjoying their quaint town, gorgeous forest, and breathtaking views of Lake Huron.

But during the rest of the year? Crickets

Well, not literally.

It was even too cold for them during winter.

Chloe went down the steps, treading carefully with her boots just in case there was a new layer of ice. Out of habit, she walked the extra block toward the water, so she could enjoy the view before she turned west toward the town square and the Hummingbird and Bluebell Inn. She'd worked at the bed-and-breakfast for almost six years, ever since she moved to Sanctuary Island. She enjoyed serving the guests, but since she'd convinced Marissa to use the kitchen for catering orders as well, that was her favorite part of the job. And also the whole reason she even had hours to put in today.

The inn, usually referred to as just "The Bluebell" by locals, stood directly on town square, the gilded sign in the yard proudly helping tourists confirm it was the place they were looking for. As one of the original houses of the founding Harlowe family, it was a gorgeous piece of history. Even with the bare bushes and snow-covered yard, The Bluebell was impressive. Chloe loved the cheery yellow paint and clean, white trim.

The two-story porch reminded her of the grand houses of Savannah or Charleston. The lower-level rooms had private access to lush garden patios in the summer, but the upper rooms had coveted views of the water across the square and straight down Main Street to the harbor.

Everything had already been cleared of snow here. Apparently, Keith had been up early. Ignoring the broad staircase leading up to the front door, she followed the small walkway along the edge of the building toward the back. She entered her code and pushed her way through the employee entrance, flicking on the light in the hallway. The smell of coffee greeted her greedy nose as she made her way to the kitchen.

Marissa was already inside, pouring herself a cup of coffee. "Morning, Chloe! Isn't it a gorgeous day?" Marissa was a naturally warm woman, built for charming guests and building friendships. She and Keith owned and operated the inn, though Keith also worked for the ferry during the season and did odd jobs around town during the winter.

"Good morning," Chloe returned the greeting as she slipped her apron over her head. After tying the apron, she turned to grab the large cup of steaming coffee Marissa had poured for her. The first sip tingled in her mouth, the liquid spreading to her stomach and awakening her senses. She closed her eyes, taking a deep breath before setting the mug down again and turning to look at the task sheet she'd prepared for the order when it had come through.

"You know anything about this order?" she asked

with a raised eyebrow. It was odd to get a catering order in the winter, let alone one for a charcuterie board and spinach artichoke puffs. The locals on the island were far more likely to order pulled pork or her famous chicken salad. Whoever Shaun Prentiss was, he certainly wasn't from around here.

"Some real estate developer from the mainland is meeting with the mayor. He ordered it to be delivered to the mayor's office. My cousin Julie said the mayor is pretty flustered about the meeting."

Chloe wasn't surprised that her boss knew the rest of the story. Marissa's family had been on the island since it was founded in the 1800s, which meant she tended to know everything that was going on around town.

She grumbled, unable to bite back her irritation at the news. "Great. Just what this town needs—some rich guy coming in and stealing up land. I hope Mayor DeBruin tells him to kick rocks."

Marissa looked at her with a raised eyebrow, but Chloe simply turned to the fridge. In six years, she hadn't shared with her boss exactly what brought her to Sanctuary Island, and she wasn't planning on doing so now. Her life was far better when she could forget Derrick Webster even existed. Which honestly wasn't as often as she'd like. The man had a bad habit of creeping into the news or her social media feed.

Squaring her shoulders, she started pulling meat and cheese out of the fridge. She'd special ordered the supplies for this charcuterie board the last time Marissa's husband took his truck across the ice bridge to the mainland. Last-minute catering jobs were almost impossible this time of year. She was thankful they had Island Market for basic groceries, but the selection sometimes made her little chef's heart cry.

With the ferry closed for the season, logistics became the hardest part of her job. The ice bridge usually formed in late December, giving them a much-needed connection for a few winter months. But just last week, that option had disappeared with a stretch of warm March days. Sanctuary was cut off again, except by plane, until the ferry could run again.

"Maybe don't let the investor see that particular attitude tomorrow morning," Marissa mused.

Chloe whirled. "What?"

Mirth danced in her boss's eyes. "Oh, didn't I mention? He's also our guest tonight. I told you we had a reservation. Breakfast for two is on the menu."

Well at least the rich jerk had the decency to spend some money while he was on the island instead of flying back out after his meeting. Heaven knew she could use the money. Marissa paid her generously, but the off-season was always tight. And she couldn't exactly expect to get paid when there was nothing to cook. She had a strong social media following and taught virtual cooking classes, but the healthy savings she'd brought with her to Sanctuary were slowly depleting.

"I'll behave," she promised. She could make breakfast for the land grabber and his wife without losing her cool.

Marissa chatted a little more as Chloe sliced the salami and then carefully folded it and prosciutto into attractive swirls across the board.

"Did you hear about Nate Hawthorne and that ballerina? I'm so happy for him. I never understood why you basically ignored the man." Marissa was in her late-fifties and happily married, but that didn't stop her from keeping tabs on every single man and woman on Sanctuary Island.

Chloe rolled her eyes. She had formed a connection with Harper, the ballerina in question, since she'd arrived, but it was still a new friendship, just a few short conversations at quilting circle. Nate was a good man, and the single dad certainly deserved whatever happiness he'd found.

But the times she'd met him, it had been obvious there was no spark, much to Marissa's dismay. What Chloe hadn't shared with her boss was that she was pretty sure whatever little piece of a heart even made sparks happen–hers was permanently broken.

Damaged beyond repair by a certain spoiled millionaire six years ago.

Of course, if it hadn't been for Derrick, she wouldn't be in Sanctuary. Not just because it had been their breakup that had sent her world into a tailspin, but because he'd talked so much about the island while they were dating. He'd fondly mentioned the summer vacations his family had spent here on more than one occasion. So, when she needed somewhere to escape, it seemed like the perfect place.

Besides, Derrick adamantly refused to visit the island since his parents died when he was a teenager. It didn't hurt that she was completely confident that she wouldn't run into him here.

She'd expected the beauty and the slow pace based on Derrick's descriptions. She hadn't expected the way she was instantly welcomed by the locals or the way she'd quickly felt like she belonged.

She hadn't expected to feel Jesus slowly pursue her during her first year here or to feel safe and secure in His presence on this tiny speck of land that most people had never heard of. Whoever had named Sanctuary Island a hundred and fifty years ago must have been prophetic.

It was her sanctuary.

Which was why she had such a visceral reaction to the idea that some greedy developer would come in and ruin all the wonderful charm and local hospitality.

A piece of sharp cheddar crumbled in her fingers as her grip tightened at the thought. Whoops. She popped the broken piece in her mouth and grabbed another, carefully adding it to the already fanned pieces on the board.

She would do whatever it took to make sure the real estate developer didn't find success here on the island. She'd make his life miserable if she had to. But his food would be perfect.

two

DERRICK

Derrick Webster steepled his fingers under his chin. It seemed like even the delicious spread on the table wasn't going to save this meeting, despite the way his meeting companion had been reaching for more every minute or so.

Across the table sat Mayor James DeBruin. He'd been mayor on Sanctuary Island for almost fifteen years. Derrick had done his research, of course. He was nothing if not methodical and strategic. And at this moment, there was nothing more strategic than locking in this development on Sanctuary Island. As much as Derrick had fought against the need to come here, he knew it was the best business decision.

He had the capital. He even had the building plans. The last piece of the puzzle was locking in the town support and purchasing the land. Lodging permits, a few extra roads, maybe a few tax breaks, and clearance to build above the town's ridiculous three-story building height restriction would go a long way to convincing the board of directors that this was the right choice. And town support would convince Travis Beekman to sell. That and the hundreds of thousands Derrick would be forking over for the land.

All the pieces would fall into place.

But Mayor DeBruin didn't seem convinced. "We've had some interest over the years from folks like you, Mr. Webster. Why exactly should the town allow Webster Hotels to build a huge resort when we've denied so many others?" He popped a cracker in his mouth, crumbs falling to the front of his department store dress shirt.

Derrick fought the urge to shift in his seat, reaching for a crumb-free piece of cheese instead. He didn't eat it, choosing instead to hold onto it as he responded. "Respectfully, my vision is different from the others. I want to turn Sanctuary Island into a year-round destination. I've seen those other proposals."

Ignoring the microscopic hint of surprise on the mayor's features, he continued, "None of them offered what I am proposing. An indoor water park, bowling alley, and movie theater along with outdoor snow tubing and snowmobile rentals. I've been in town for two hours, Mr. DeBruin, and even I can see that Sanctuary is struggling along until May. But it doesn't have to be like that."

Derrick didn't reveal his personal connection to Sanctuary Island. Not that it mattered. Emotion had no place in business, and he would have a hard enough time convincing the board of directors that this wasn't an emotional investment. No, it was a strategic decision based on the potential of this undiscovered gem in Lake Huron.

It was going to be the perfect place for Webster Hotels to place the first of his new line of family-friendly resorts. He just had to get the local government on board. He took a small bite from the corner of the cheese. The creamy texture enveloped his palate, melting delicately like velvet under the warmth of his tongue. There was butteriness and subtle tanginess that lingered in his mouth. It was, most of all, an unexpected luxury from this island that was still only accessible by plane until the spring.

"We happen to like Sanctuary Island just the way it is, Mr. Webster." Mayor DeBruin shifted in his chair, his back more rigid than it had been a moment ago. Apparently, he hadn't liked hearing the truth about the economics of his little town.

"It's a lovely little place," Derrick placated. "Obviously, we don't want to take away from the history of the place or the..." he searched for the right word, "*quaintness* of the locale. Family Adventure Resorts will bring many year-round jobs to the island, along with an influx of new and repeat visitors who can fall in love with the charm of the island."

Nailed it. Derrick was pleased with his argument, but his confidence slipped as the mayor's frown only deepened.

Derrick leaned forward, resting his elbows on the table but keeping his hands open in front of him, always conscious of the body language of negotiation. "What do you need from me to be convinced that Family Adventure Resorts and Webster Hotels are a good choice for Sanctuary Island?"

Mayor DeBruin pressed his lips together. "That's an excellent question, Mr. Webster. You talk a good game, and I have to admit to feeling slightly outmatched. I think I need a more complete picture of what this resort will look like. How does it function? How many guests? Logistics for travel. And all the other details, of course."

Derrick bit the inside of his cheek but didn't let his frustration show on his face. "Of course. How about we have another meeting next week, and I'll have a more formal presentation set up?"

"I'll have Julie set it up."

The men rose from the table and shook hands. Derrick had been hoping for a warmer reception to the proposal today, but what Mayor DeBruin was asking for wasn't unreasonable. He gathered his mostly unused papers from the table.

"Oh, and Mr. Webster?"

Derrick glanced up at the mayor.

"Next meeting, we'll have you present to the entire Sanctuary Island Community Advisory Board."

"Oh?" Derrick couldn't bite back his surprise this time.

DeBruin gave a small chuckle. "I'm just one man, Mr. Webster. I try not to make decisions in a vacuum. If my advisory board votes in favor of your development, then I'll follow their recommendation. But if they don't…"

Derrick nodded sharply as the mayor trailed off, leaving the implication hanging in the air. Impressing the advisory board was suddenly priority number one. But he didn't know anything about them or their goals. He'd have to have his assistant, Shaun, get as much information as possible before their first meeting.

If wooing the town advisory board was part of the mission, then he'd gladly do it. Which also meant he'd be staying in Sanctuary until this was settled. He could do a good amount of information gathering while he stayed. And it wasn't like the bed-and-breakfast wouldn't have room. The place was a ghost town.

"I'll look forward to meeting the board and showing them the potential of this investment."

Mayor DeBruin showed him out, and Derrick gave a friendly nod to the woman at the desk near the exit. She flashed him a broad smile and tucked her hair behind her ear. He racked his brain for her name. Jenny? Jamie?

"Julie, we need a meeting on the schedule with SICAB and Mr. Webster here." The mayor pronounced the acronym 'sigh-cab'.

"Of course. I'll get it set up immediately."

"Thank you. I better get back to work," the mayor said. "See you next week, Mr. Webster."

He shook Mr. DeBruin's hand again before the man disappeared back into his office, probably to polish off the rest of the charcuterie board. Derrick was absently wishing he'd had another piece of that cheese before he left.

With her boss gone, Julie turned her attention to Derrick. "Will you be staying in town until the meeting, Mr. Webster? I'd be happy to show you around."

He saw the interest in her eyes and couldn't miss the invitation in her words. "I'll be staying, but I think I'll mostly be working. Wouldn't want to make any mistakes when I present to the board," he added with a wink to soften the blow of rejection.

Julie giggled and batted her eyes at him. "You know what they say about all work and no play, Mr. Webster?"

It makes Jack a billionaire, he wanted to reply. Almost-billionaire, he corrected. Instead of indulging her flirtation any further, he simply offered one last tight smile. "My assistant, Shaun, has my schedule. I believe you already have his contact information?"

Julie nodded. "Of course. I'll take care of it. I'm happy to take care of absolutely *anything* you need while you're on the island."

Derrick nearly winced at her overt come-on, a reaction tempered by the familiarity of such advances. His financial success came with its own set of predictable interactions, and while he was used to the attention, it didn't make it any less uncomfortable. It was time to get out of here.

"I think I can manage. Have a good day, Julie."

Once he pushed through the door of the small-town hall building, the crisp winter air was a welcome relief. The cold wind felt invigorating against his skin, clearing his mind from the cloying atmosphere inside. Derrick took a deep breath, appreciating the brief moment of solitude before he had to dive back into the whirlwind of responsibilities that awaited him.

If success was riding on his meeting with SICAB next week, he was going to do everything in his power to make sure it was successful. He pulled out his phone and dialed Shaun.

Shaun had been his assistant for nearly four years. After a string of women who were more interested in finding their spot on his social calendar than managing his professional one, he had been especially grateful for the day the young, well-dressed college student had appeared in his office.

So far, Shaun was completely unflappable.

"Hey, boss."

"We're done. Where are you?"

"I tried to find a coffee shop, but the closest thing I could find open in the afternoon was this cupcake place. Turns out they don't even have seating. So I'm outside on the bench."

"Got it." Derrick hung up without listening for any other info, knowing exactly where Shaun had ended up.

Derrick headed east until he was greeted by the iconic pink-and-blue awning he remembered. Nearly twenty years later and it looked mostly the same. Cathy's Cupcakes had been a favorite destination for his family way back then, and it seemed to have stood the test of time.

Shaun had settled on a small bench outside the

cupcake shop. Shaun looked up at him through his thin-framed glasses, one raised eyebrow the only hint of the questions lurking inside. Perhaps Derrick should be a little more subtle with his familiarity of the island. After all, no one here knew he'd been here before. Not a soul on the island would remember him, and his team couldn't suspect why this was so important to him.

"You found it," Shaun mused.

The wooden bench groaned as he sat. "This town has like forty residents this time of year. You think *cupcakes* doesn't narrow it down enough for Google to get me to the right place?"

Shaun just blinked at him and turned back to the computer balanced on his lap. Derrick wasn't sure if he was convinced, but his assistant was smart enough not to push any more.

Derrick glanced at the door, noting the off-season hours posted on the glass. Only two days a week. Not for long, if he had his way. His Family Adventure resort would boost Cathy's business enough to have her working full hours, even in March.The bells over the door jingled cheerily as someone stepped outside.

The smell of vanilla and sugar wafted out, his mouth watering.

"Come on, let's go find a place to sit inside. There's a café up the street."

They stepped inside the Eastside Café, the worn linoleum floors slippery under his feet as the snow clinging to his dress shoes melted in the warmth.

"We need to extend our reservation. Next week–" Derrick was cut off by a woman standing in front of them.

"Welcome to Eastside. Grab a seat anywhere. Do you want coffee?"

Derrick was surveying the dining room and didn't respond.

"I'll take a hot tea," Shaun replied quickly.

The women shifted her eyes to Derrick. "What about you? Do you want coffee? Or are you a tea drinker like your friend here?"

It was obvious from the woman's voice that she didn't approve of Shaun's beverage choice.

"Coffee, black," Derrick confirmed with a smile. *Operation: Charm the Locals* was officially underway. Which meant he'd drink a cup of coffee, even though it was nearly 4 PM and he was likely to be up half the night because of it.

She flashed him a smile and glared at Shaun.

"Making friends already, are you?" he asked his assistant with amusement. He walked to a booth in the corner.

Shaun ignored his comment, but followed and sat across from him. "So next week?"

"Right. We're staying until at least next week. We have a presentation with the community advisory board, and the mayor's approval is dependent on their recommendation."

Shaun nodded, pulling out his phone. Likely to take notes. The man was meticulous, and Derrick appreciated every single obsessive tendency.

He ticked off a few more key points on his fingers, including the basic framework he wanted to use for the presentation. Shaun tapped away on his phone the whole time, and when Derrick wrapped up his initial thoughts, his assistant looked up and waited for more.

"That's it for now. We're here for a week. I need to know everything about the members of the advisory board. Which means I need you to stop ticking off the locals and make friends," he said with a pointed glance at Shaun's mug with a tea bag dunked in it.

Shaun's calm expression broke. "How was I supposed to know ordering tea was a cardinal sin? It's on the menu!"

Derrick held a serious glare for a moment longer, before he couldn't hold back the smile. "I'm just messing with you. Well, not actually about the making friends part. We need every advantage we can get. And around here? Information is power and connections are everything."

"Got it. Let's go check into the bed-and-breakfast

and we'll extend our reservation when we get there. And then you can buy me dinner to make up for the one I have to cancel with Jessica for tomorrow night. You know, since you *promised* we'd leave tomorrow." Shaun rolled his eyes and gave Derrick a wry smile, one corner of his mouth turning up in resignation.

"Send her flowers with my card," Derrick offered.

"Perfect. They'll go great with the dinner I have being delivered for her."

Derrick smiled. Shaun's devotion to his girlfriend was unflagging. Derrick hadn't felt that way about anyone since… He shook his head to push away the thoughts of her. "You can use my card for that, too."

"Oh, I planned on it."

Derrick barked a laugh. "I think you're a little too comfortable in your position, Shaun."

Another raised eyebrow from his unflappable assistant. "Go ahead and fire me. I'm sure Julie from the mayor's office will be happy to step in and handle anything you need."

Derrick's eyes widened. "How on earth do you know that? Did you have your mobster uncle string a wire into my suit jacket?" He made a show of checking his lapel.

Shaun chuckled. "No, but that's not a bad idea. After all, the only time things fall through the cracks are when you forget to tell me something. I can cut out the middleman."

"Har har har," Derrick said drily.

"Julie just emailed," he said, gesturing to his computer screen. "She seems very accommodating."

Derrick groaned. "What did she say?"

Shaun's amusement at Derrick's misery was obvious. "She wanted to reiterate her invitation for a private tour of the island, ending with a home-cooked meal at her house."

Derrick muttered under his breath. "Handle it." His voice left no room for argument and hopefully made it very clear to Shaun that he wasn't amused by the woman's antics.

"Yes, boss."

"But don't make her angry. The last thing I need is an enemy within the mayor's office." Derrick could only imagine the havoc that Julie could wreak if she felt slighted.

Shaun scoffed. "Mr. Webster, please. One of my most practiced skills is diplomatically disappointing the women vying for a place at your side."

"A place near my bank account, you mean."

"If you say so, sir."

Derrick sighed. Shaun might be the closest thing he had to a friend, but he wasn't actually a friend. At the end of the day, Mr. Prentiss was still only his assistant.

Position and wealth like his didn't really allow for many friendships. Or relationships.

He'd been down that road before, and it had ended with the engagement ring and a scribbled note left on the counter of his Chicago penthouse. Relationships were out of the question.

three

CHLOE

Chloe prided herself on keeping the cleanest kitchen on the island. After she prepped everything for breakfast the next morning, she wiped everything down until the stainless-steel worktable was gleaming. Then, she set the table in the dining room.

Wood-stained tables scattered the large room, between two and six chairs at each table, allowing guests to either dine alone or mingle with others. It was a cozy spot for tourists to have a warm, freshly cooked breakfast before they went out to explore and enjoy the island. She inhaled the fresh wood smell of the fire burning at one end of the attached sitting room.

She set the main table with a delicate touch, arranging vintage floral china plates at each setting, accompanied by polished silverware and linen napkins neatly folded. Mismatched teacups added a charming and personal touch. Chloe ensured that every detail was perfect, from the positioning of the cups and saucers to the alignment of the bread plates, creating a picturesque scene for the guests. Even if there were only two guests tonight, they'd have the full experience.

Since they'd ordered the charcuterie tray earlier in the day, she couldn't use that for the afternoon hors d'oeuvres. She kept small portions of her homemade dips frozen for instances just like this, and quickly put together a spread of caramelized onion dip and pita chips for the guests to snack on before dinner.

Chloe surveyed her handiwork with a careful eye, straightening a few pieces before retreating into the kitchen. Voices drifted from the foyer as Marissa greeted their guests and checked them in.

She couldn't make out any words, but the voice stopped her in her tracks. No, it couldn't be him. It wasn't possible.

A door closed and she risked a peek down the hallway from her kitchen door, sagging in relief as she saw a tall, slim man standing next to Marissa's guest desk. He was far too young to be Derrick. And Derrick would never wear the floral print button-down and old-fashioned flat cap this man was wearing. It was very fashion-forward and completely out of place in Sanctuary. His wife must have stepped into the restroom, since he was standing there alone, but at least her heart could start beating again.

She stepped back into the kitchen, shaking away her anxiety with a laugh. She was being ridiculous. Derrick Webster wouldn't come to Sanctuary Island, let alone in the middle of winter. He was more the hut-suspended-over-the-ocean-in-the-Maldives kind of guy.

Not that she'd ever seen him take a vacation. Not in the two years they'd been together. Not even when she'd eventually planned one for the both of them and he'd canceled at the last minute, leaving her holding her bag and marching slowly down the steps of his private jet, fighting back tears. It had been that moment that solidified what she'd already known. Derrick Webster would always put work first.

Chloe took a deep breath and took one last glance around the kitchen. Marissa would clear the hor d'oeuvres tonight, and Chloe would be back bright and early to fix breakfast for the surprisingly young investor and his wife.

Stepping into the hallway, she turned away from the reception desk and walked to the back door. She walked toward the harbor, enjoying the quiet of the town square. Living somewhere without cars allowed in most of the town had taken some getting used to, but now she could appreciate what the town had been thinking all those years ago. During the hardest part of winter, snowmobiles were a common sight, navigating the snow-packed streets. And in the summer? Horse-drawn carriages, bicycles, and lots and lots of tourists on foot.

She knew the tourists were important to the island. There were tons of businesses that even quit operating during the off-season because it wasn't even worth staffing. No town of 700 people needed fourteen restaurants. But in the summer? Every single one would have a wait each night.

Tonight, she was meeting her friends for dinner at Fresh Catch. It was a quick jaunt across the town square, which was really a circle. But when she'd tried to call it the town circle during her first few months here, Marissa had laughed for two minutes straight.

The sprawling white one-story building had a large deck facing the water. During the summer, she hardly attempted to come here, as it was one of the most popular restaurants. Which was why they'd chosen it tonight for her dinner with Angelica and Jo. Plus, their friend Lisa owned it. And while she'd be slightly preoccupied, they could usually rope her into the conversation at some point in the evening.

A quick glance around the dining room revealed that her friends weren't here yet. She waved at Lisa, who was taking orders at another table.

"Grab whatever table you want," her friend called across the restaurant.

Chloe grabbed a table and slung her purse over the chair, glancing around the dining room.

Paul Solheim was there with Rummy Fielding—Angie's uncle whom she'd lived with since she was a teenager–and they brightened at the sight of her.

"Chloe! Come on over here," Paul hollered.

Chloe's heart sang. This was what she loved about Sanctuary. She'd lived in Chicago for fifteen years and had never been greeted with such warmth and familiarity when she saw an acquaintance on the street.

"Hey there, Paul. How are you doing tonight?"

"You heard anything about this hoity-toity investor in town?"

Chloe raised an eyebrow. News sure spread quickly in this small town. And gossip spread even faster.

"I don't know anything." She laughed, putting her hands in the air in surrender.

Rummy harrumphed. "I was talking to Jimmy this afternoon. Said he wants the committee to listen to this guy's spiel and give a recommendation."

Chloe knew that Rummy was talking about James DeBruin, the mayor. But when you'd lived here as long as Rummy, apparently you were on a nickname basis with even the mayor. She was still too nervous around him to call him anything but Mr. Mayor, despite the number of times he'd asked her to call him Jimmy.

"I'm glad he's asking SICAB to do that," she said honestly. The last thing she wanted was the mayor blinded by the dollar signs.

The image of the investor at the front desk of the inn flashed through her mind. The committee was going to despise his casual hipster style. If that was what he'd worn to a meeting with the mayor, the old-fashioned members of the committee would be less than impressed.

"I still can't believe I got nominated for the committee last year," she admitted.

Coming up beside her, Angelica scoffed. "You're exactly what that committee needed, Chloe. Buncha old farts stuck in the 80s without you there to bring them into this millennium." Angelica turned to the table with a mischievous twinkle in her eye. "Oh, Rummy, didn't see you there."

Chloe chuckled and Rummy's lips twitched. "Watch it, missy." He turned back to Chloe. "Go on, enjoy your dinner. I'll see you at the next meeting and we'll figure out what this city-slicker wants with our little island anyway."

Chloe said good-bye to Raymond and Paul, then showed Angie the table she'd claimed by the window. It would be a little chilly, but the view of the sunset over the water was worth it. They were joined by Jo Fletcher a few minutes later, looking slightly frazzled. Her long blond hair was pulled back, and a few strands had escaped in the wind.

"Sorry, I had to get Sam settled with Gail."

Jo's daughter Samantha was seven and Chloe absolutely adored her. Gail Olsen was the pastor's wife, and she often helped Jo out by keeping an eye on Sam.

Chloe spotted Harper craning her neck near the entrance and stood up to wave her over, sure to confirm she knew the other ladies at the table as well.

Conversation quickly took off, and before she knew it, Lisa was clearing their plates from the table. Dinner with her friends was exactly what Chloe needed, but she couldn't stay too late. Marissa had texted her to let her know the guests had asked for breakfast at 7 AM, which meant Chloe would be at the inn by six to prepare everything.

She said good-bye and quickly walked home, bracing herself against the cold night. The town's old-fashioned streetlights lit her way, and despite the chill, Chloe was struck with the same overwhelming sense of peace and contentment she'd become familiar with since moving here.

The next morning, Chloe danced across the kitchen at The Bluebell, humming softly to herself as she carried the dishes to the counter to be plated. She tied on a fresh apron, refusing to appear in front of guests with avocado smeared on her front. She heard Marissa greet someone, and noise from the living room filtered through the cracked door between the kitchen and the dining space.

She opened the door and saw the man from yesterday afternoon. "Good morning, Mr. Prentiss. I'm Chloe and I'm your chef this morning. Please help yourself to coffee and juice." She gestured to the side table where the beverages were already set up. "There are also fresh baked muffins on the table."

Mr. Prentiss looked at her with wide-eyes but didn't say anything. What was wrong with this guy?

"Okay, well… I'll be in the kitchen putting the finishing touches on breakfast and I'll have it out for you in just a few minutes."

She disappeared into the kitchen.

Ignoring the awkward exchange, she focused on the food. She placed a perfectly poached egg on a bed of sautéed spinach, its yolk ready to ooze out at the slightest touch. Beside it, she arranged a slice of toasted sourdough bread topped with ripe avocado and a sprinkle of sea salt and chili flakes. A few roasted cherry tomatoes added a burst of color and sweetness, while a hearty serving of thick-cut bacon would bring a homey touch. To complete the dish, Chloe added a heavy drizzle of hollandaise sauce over the egg. Her own plate would have had even more, but not everyone wanted their food drowning in sauce.

The meal was simple and indulgent, which was her signature style. She couldn't deny the hint of imposter syndrome that was creeping up her spine at the thought of some hipster rich guy critiquing her food, but she squared her shoulders and shook off the feeling. She had worked at some of the fanciest restaurants in Chicago before moving here, and her food earned rave reviews on all the travel blogs and review sites.

Chloe glanced back out the door to see if Mrs. Prentiss had joined her husband yet. She caught her gasp of surprise when another man was seated at the table with the young real estate mogul. Oh. She could only see the back of his head, but he appeared to be quite a bit taller than Mr. Prentiss, with broad shoulders and a dusting of gray in his short-trimmed hair.

Well, that was unexpected, but she'd get their breakfast and be thankful the man hadn't come in while she was having an already uncomfortable exchange with Mr. Prentiss.

Chloe grabbed the plates and pushed through the swinging kitchen door.

"Good morning, everyone." The guests turned their attention to Chloe as she spoke. "I've prepared one of my favorite—"

The dishes clattered to the floor as piercing green eyes met hers. She froze like Lake Huron in January.

"Chloe," Marissa's too-cheerful voice called out, "is everything okay?"

Chloe couldn't move or speak, her heart stuck permanently in her throat.

"Oh my goodness." Marissa's shocked voice jerked Chloe back to the present.

She ripped her gaze from Derrick Webster's shocked gaze and turned her attention to the mess on the floor.

Marissa recovered quickly. "I'm so sorry, everyone. Please enjoy the muffins and coffee while we get this cleaned up and fresh plates made up."

Marissa was practically screaming at Chloe with the forceful expression in her eyes, urging her into the kitchen. In a daze, she picked up the plates, which had thankfully bounced on her rubber-soled shoes and not broken. She bee-lined for the safety of the kitchen, away from Derrick's penetrating stare.

Marissa had gathered a handful of food with her hands and followed Chloe into the kitchen. She tossed it on the counter, planting a hand on her hips. "What on earth, Chloe? Are you okay?"

Chloe buried her face in her hands. This couldn't be happening. Why was he here with another investor?

And then the answer to her own question made her groan. Of course. He *was* the investor.

"I'm going to go wipe up the mess in the dining room, and you are going to plate two more breakfasts." Marissa's no-nonsense tone settled Chloe's heart rate. "Do you have enough food?"

Chloe tore her thoughts away from the man in the other room and the way her heart all but cracked open, leaking out on the floor like the poached eggs.

Food. Breakfast.

She blinked, trying to think. "I need to poach new eggs. But otherwise, I have enough."

Chloe shoved all her thoughts about Derrick into a box in the corner of her mind. Then, she slammed the lid and turned the key, turning her focus to fixing the giant mess she'd made of this breakfast.

Marissa came in and out as she wiped the floor and cleared the food scraps. Chloe could feel her curious gaze, but she ignored her boss. When she'd successfully poached two more eggs, she replated the meals.

"Ready," she announced, looking to Marissa. "Can you take them out?"

Marissa raised an eyebrow. "Seriously? You love serving the guests."

"Not these guests," Chloe said flippantly, then wishing she hadn't when her friend's eyebrow nearly hit her hairline. “Please, Marissa?” she pleaded in a whisper.

She couldn’t go out there and face Derrick, pretending everything was okay.

“Fine,” Marissa agreed. “But you’re going to tell me what this is all about eventually, okay?”

Chloe nodded, shoulders sagging in relief at not having to face what was waiting for her in the dining room–the past.

four

DERRICK

DERRICK HADN'T STOPPED STARING AT THE DOOR SINCE IT closed behind her. The woman he'd assumed he would never see again had floated across the floor, elegant as ever in her clean white chef's apron and a friendly smile on her face. Until she'd seen him.

How was she even here? Why would Chloe be working at The Hummingbird and Bluebell? She had been one of the highest rated up-and-coming chefs in Chicago when they broke up. And yet, here she was on Sanctuary Island.

Nothing about this made sense.

The door swung open, causing his heart to skip. But it was just the older woman who had checked them in. The manager? It didn't matter. Right now, he only cared that she wasn't Chloe.

"Uhhh, boss?"

Derrick tore his eyes away from the door, finding Shaun studying him carefully. With a deep breath, he flipped into professional mode. Whatever Chloe was doing here, he wasn't going to let it derail his plans.

"What is it, Shaun?"

His assistant's eyes flickered. "You're not going to explain what that was?"

"What do you mean?" Derrick was careful to keep his tone casual and unaffected—despite being anything but.

Shaun gave a knowing hum. "So that's how you want to play it."

Derrick turned to the muffin in front of him. He was normally more careful about sugar and carbs, but after the unexpected appearance of his ex this morning, he deserved some extra calories in the form of baked goods.

It was light and sweet, with a slight crunch from the sugar on the top. Perfect.

Which only made him think of the woman who had baked it. The moist muffin turned to sawdust in his mouth. He set it aside, gulping down his juice.

"Did you get our reservation extended?" Derrick changed the subject, desperate to think about anything other than Chloe Bennett. His glance slid back to the wall that separated them from the kitchen. After all these years, she was here.

A flush of anger filled him. What right did she have to come to Sanctuary Island? Of course, he'd mentioned it to her. She was probably the only person in the world who knew what the island meant to him. How dare she take it from him?

"Boss?"

Derrick belatedly looked up from the muffin he was slowly mangling with his butter knife. Shaun looked at him expectantly. Apparently, he'd missed whatever his assistant had been saying.

"What are my options?" The question was one he asked often, pushing to get more information from his employees when they came to him for an opinion. He was hoping it would be enough to get some context for whatever Shaun had been asking him.

Shaun, however, knew him better than that. "Like I said, we can stay here for the entire stay, or we can check out some of the other island accommodations. There is some sort of resort."

"The Palace," Derrick murmured, almost to himself.

Shaun quirked an eyebrow. "The Shore View Palace, yes. Perhaps the closest competition for—"

"We'll stay here," Derrick decided.

"Yes, sir," his assistant replied. There were a hundred unasked questions in those words, but Shaun was too perceptive to push.

"The Shore View is closed during the off-season," he added, as though that were the reason for his decision.

Derrick turned back to his muffin, silently kicking himself for being so impulsive. Why would he want to stay here? Clearly, he wasn't thinking straight. Of course, Chloe had always had that effect on him. Wanting to spend time with her had almost cost him some of the biggest deals of his career. It had been for the best that she'd ended it.

He should tell Shaun he changed his mind. Surely there was another bed and breakfast on the island. But that would probably only bring more questions from his astute assistant. Derrick didn't change his mind—ever. And he certainly wouldn't be changing it because of Chloe. He was going to get to the bottom of why she was here on the island though.

The door swung open again, but it was the manager bringing them their replated breakfast. His lips twitched at the memory. Leave it to Chloe to drop two full plates of food on the floor at the sight of him. He was kind of surprised she hadn't immediately marched back in here and confronted him, though. She'd always been a firecracker.

It was probably only a matter of time.

The plate before him looked amazing, which wasn't surprising at all. She was an amazing chef. Which, again, begged the question... why was she here on

Sanctuary Island when the last vestiges of winter were still clinging to the island? Maybe during the busy summer season he could see her working at The Lantern Room, which was the most expensive, high-end restaurant on the island. Or, at least, it had been back when he was a teenager. His parents had always tried to have one dinner there during each visit. Sometimes, Derrick had stayed with a babysitter they hired. But the last year they'd come, he went with them.

Guilt filled him with memory. He'd been a sulky teenager, all but ruining their dinner because he'd wanted to go out with friends for pizza instead.

If he could go back…

He shook the thought from his mind and focused on his breakfast, along with his agenda for the next week. "First order of business, we need to find out more about this advisory board the mayor mentioned. Any ideas where to start?"

Shaun straightened, waving a piece of bacon in one hand as he answered. "Actually, yeah. I was thinking about it last night. I think it's time you got a haircut, boss."

Derrick's hand immediately went to his hair, which was nowhere near due for a trim. He furrowed his brow at his assistant. "Explain."

Shaun grinned. "If I learned anything growing up in Minden, Indiana, it's that the one person who knows everything that happens in a small town is the local hair stylist."

Derrick's smile widened slightly. He picked up his own bacon and pointed it at Shaun. "That's brilliant."

Shaun shrugged. "I know. So, about that raise..."

Derrick smirked. "Nice try. We both know I already pay you the salary of a manager."

"It was worth a shot."

The door opened once more, revealing the manager bringing in a new carafe of coffee. Derrick's thoughts were pulled once more to the woman he knew must be on the other side. The phone rang from the reception desk in the hall and the manager left the dining room using another door. He glanced back at the closed kitchen door. If Chloe wasn't going to face this like an adult, then he would.

"Just a second," he said, excusing himself from the table.

Derrick rapped a knuckle on the door a moment before pushing it slowly open. "Chloe, I—"

A quick glance around the kitchen confirmed what he felt the instant he'd opened the door. She was gone.

His jaw clenched, and his hand fell to his side. He shoved the fist into his pocket, ignoring the frustration and disappointment that filled him with the knowledge that she had run away.

He sucked in a breath. Good riddance. It wasn't like

he was going to kick her off the island. But if she didn't want to talk, then they wouldn't talk. He had as good of a poker face as anyone.

She was the one who'd broken things off anyway. She'd run away before, and now she'd run away again. It had been for the best. Logically, he knew that. But it didn't make it sting any less when he'd returned from closing the deal in Omaha expecting to celebrate with his fiancée only to find every trace of her removed from his condo.

That had certainly been a slap in the face. Whatever pride and excitement he'd had about the deal had disappeared at the sight of her ring on the counter. But if she didn't want to be with him, he wasn't going to beg.

So, he'd moved on.

Never to another woman. Being CEO of Webster Hotels took all his time and focus. And he was never going to let a woman make him feel guilty for handling his responsibilities. He thought Chloe understood, but he'd been wrong.

As he returned to the table, Shaun studied his every move. Derrick snapped his napkin. His jaw clenched as he tried to disguise his frustration.

"Chloe, huh?"

"Don't even," he warned him. "It's ancient history."

"Well, if it's ancient, then maybe she can—"

"What are you doing while I get my haircut today?" he asked, cutting him off.

Shaun sighed, apparently resigned to the fact that Derrick wasn't going to tell him more. "I'm going to visit the chamber of commerce, get a feel for the businesses in town, and work on your presentation."

Derrick nodded. "Good. We can meet back at lunch and see where we stand."

He mopped up one last bit of the poached egg using the avocado toast. At least staying here would mean a good breakfast. Maybe he'd figure out how to ignore that he was once in love with the woman cooking it. And maybe she wouldn't poison it. The bite he'd taken lodged in his throat at the thought that he was definitely not Chloe's favorite person. She'd probably spit in his food once she realized who it was for.

Well, she was going to have to get over it. It was just business—then and now.

five

CHLOE

Chloe had walked across town square at least four times, weaving through the adjacent streets like a woman on a mission. But she was the opposite. She was tied up in knots, angry and shocked. And worst of all, she was avoiding the one place she should actually be.

She'd actually walked out on Marissa. The dishes were undone and there was still food on the counter. Derrick and the other man had barely received their breakfast plates when Chloe bolted. Marissa was practically a saint, but Chloe wasn't sure exactly how she was going to explain this away.

"Oh don't worry, boss. It's only my millionaire ex-fiancé staying at the inn. He destroyed all my hopes and dreams and left me an empty shell of a woman. And now that I'm finally happy and whole after six years on

Sanctuary Island, I'm terrified that he's here to take it all away, too."

Yep, that sounded like a totally normal and not at all emotionally damaging conversation. The text message she'd sent her boss had been almost laughable, if she hadn't been so close to crying.

CB: I'm so sorry. I'm fine. I'll be back later.

The whole situation was surreal. There was a huge part of her that sort of hoped the entire thing was a bad dream. She'd looked down at her legs in the kitchen twice to make sure she was wearing pants. Seriously, all the situation needed was an embarrassing "forgot to get dressed that morning" scene to be pretty spot on with an anxiety-induced nightmare.

But no. This was all too real. And it was Derrick, as much as she'd hoped it had been some unlikely doppelganger situation. A quick call to Zach, who worked at the airport confirmed that Derrick had arrived via a private charter from the mainland the day before. Zach even insisted on calling him Mr. Webster, which made Chloe want to chuck her cell phone into a snowbank.

"Chloe!"

She whirled around at the sound of her name, saw who called it, and then immediately kept walking the opposite direction.

"Come on, Chloe. You can't ignore me forever."

"Wanna bet?" she muttered under her breath.

"I'm going to be here for a week!"

His words stopped her in her tracks. A week? No, they were checking out today. Marissa had said as much yesterday. Belatedly, she realized that Derrick's long strides meant he was now rapidly approaching the spot where she'd frozen in shock.

She pushed forward. "Go away, Derrick."

"I can't do that, Chloe."

This time, when she whipped around, Derrick was only a foot away. Her balance shifted as her heel slipped on an unmelted patch of ice hiding in the shadow of a tree. Stupid eternal winter.

Her off-balance form threatened to topple her to the sidewalk as she wobbled. She threw her hands out the side, but Derrick's strong grip on her forearm suddenly steadied her.

"Whoa there. Careful." His voice was soft, almost tender, contrasting sharply with the cold bite of the winter breeze and the painful squeeze of her chest every time she looked at him.

She glared at him, her eyes icy daggers beneath the fur-lined hood. The heat of her anger was almost enough to melt the frost from her eyelashes. "I don't need your help," she spat, yanking her arm free from his grasp. Her breath puffed out in frosty clouds, dissipating quickly in the crisp air.

Derrick's expression didn't change. He stood his

ground, his own breath mingling with hers in the chilly air. "I know you don't," he replied with a steady and calm voice. The winter wind tousled his hair, but his eyes remained locked on hers, unwavering.

She could hear the faint crunch of the snow beneath her boots as she shifted her weight, feeling the cold seep through the thin soles. The distant sound of an engine struggling to start echoed down the empty street, a reminder of how desolate and unwelcoming this season could be.

But more than the cold, it was Derrick's presence that unnerved her. The memories of warmer days, when they laughed together instead of fighting, seemed like a cruel joke now. She swallowed hard, the lump in her throat almost painful. "Why can't you just leave me alone?" she whispered, the words barely audible.

Derrick sighed, his breath a warm plume in the frigid air. "Why are you here, Saucy?" His voice held a note of pleading, a crack in his otherwise confident demeanor.

"Don't call me that. We are not friends, okay?" she said, her voice stronger now, fueled by the anger and hurt bubbling just beneath the surface.

Derrick took a step back, the crunch of snow underfoot loud in the silence that followed. He raised his hands in a gesture of surrender. "Okay, fine. But you have to admit, it's weird."

Chloe scoffed. "You showing up here after all this time... What am I doing here? I live here, Derrick. I've lived here for six years, and never once been forced to think about you." She left out the fact that just because she hadn't been forced to think about him, didn't mean that she hadn't. It would only feed his impossibly huge ego. "So, maybe the real question is what are *you* doing here?"

He hesitated for a moment, his eyes searching hers for something—understanding, forgiveness, she didn't know. Finally, he nodded. "I'm building a new development here. A family resort."

"We don't need your resort," she retorted.

Derrick looked around, extending his arms toward the empty town square. "Are you sure about that? Because from where I'm sitting, this town is desperate for something to carry it through the winter months."

Anger flooded through her, needing to defend the island she loved so much. "And what makes you think we want your help? You don't know anything about what it's like to live on this island. We're a community. We care about each other. Something you obviously know nothing about."

If the words stung, Derrick didn't show it. Beyond a slight tick in his jaw, his expression remained unchanging.

"If you would just listen," he started, but Chloe had

already tuned him out. Too many of his arguments started the same way. Derrick always had a plan, always some grand vision about the next deal. But they always ended the same way: with Chloe alone, hopes dashed, while she waited for him.

"I can tell you right now, Derrick, there is absolutely no chance your hotel or resort or whatever is getting built on this island. I will not let it happen." She felt the vow surge through her body, anchoring her in place.

Derrick flashed his signature cocky grin, and it immediately made her blood boil. But not as much as the words he said next. "And what exactly do you think you can do about it? How long have you been here again? You're not one of these people. All I'm trying to do is bring more people here, more jobs, more opportunities. Why does that make me the bad guy?"

Chloe's lips twisted. "Oh, Derrick, haven't you figured it out? You're always the bad guy."

Feeling highly satisfied with that final word, Chloe spun away and marched in the opposite direction. If Derrick and the other man were staying for another week, she had work to do.

It had been a few weeks since they had long-term guests at the inn. It would be a nice change to have the predictable routine of fixing breakfast and hors d'oeuvres every day for a bit. Her mind flicked through the other responsibilities on her plate. There were no catering orders on the docket and, other than the online cooking classes that she taught, this time of year, she had nothing but the quilting circle she was only halfway interested in.

Chloe pulled out her phone and checked her calendar. A glimmer of a smile ghosted her lips as she saw her upcoming appointment: Sanctuary Island Community Advisory Board meeting, Tuesday next week.

Replaying the conversation she had at Fresh Catch last night with Raymond and Paul, her anticipation grew.

Derrick was the investor that SICAB was voting on. And the last thing Derrick expected was Chloe to be on the board. He had said it himself. He didn't think that she belonged here, that she wasn't a local, but she knew better. Every fiber of Chloe's being belonged on this island, no matter what time of year it was. She loved the bustling summers, with the hordes of tourists arriving on the ferry each day.

She loved the smell of fresh fish in the harbor and the noise in the square from families visiting the souvenir shops and the ice cream parlor. She loved seeing the island come alive late in May. And a part of her understood why Derrick was so attached to this place. His summers growing up must've been magical here.

But what he didn't know, what most visitors to the

island didn't understand, was that during the winter, the island was no less magical. It was like the island needed to sleep after the craziness of summer. A quiet slowly crept over the land as the tourists faded away, and the first snow fell, blanketing everything for a sort of hibernation.

Sure, there were a few people who ventured out—snowmobiles or cross-country skiiers, and people who liked the adventure of crossing the ice bridge once it had formed. Which was why The Hummingbird and Bluebell Inn stayed open, just in case. But it was during the off-season that the full-time residents of Sanctuary Island really connected.

Her friends, Angie, Lisa, and Jo, were all so busy during the summer months that they barely got to see each other. Angelica was usually completely booked for her seaplane tours, and Lisa barely left the restaurant. Jo was out on fishing charters with tourists eager to reel in a big catch. And Chloe was up with the sun, serving breakfast to a full house. Thirty guests don't sound like a lot until you try to make Belgian waffles for all of them at their preferred breakfast time.

By the time the reservations slowed down, all of them were ready for a break. And the winter was long enough that by the time it ended, everyone was itching for the ferry to reopen and bring the first visitors of the season again.

Season in and season out, there was a rhythm to the island that spoke to her soul. And consistent through each cycle, she loved the way the lighthouse shone from the northeastern point every night, without fail. That was the kind of stability she needed in her life.

Whatever Derrick thought, Chloe had lived that cycle five times. She'd been welcomed to the island in a way that Derrick would never understand. Not because the island wouldn't accept him, but because he would never allow himself to put down those roots.

Any hotel that Derrick built here would just be another feather in his company's hat. A giant, corporate-run monstrosity with no soul and no concern for the impact on the island.

Which was why she had to stop him.

six

DERRICK

UNSURPRISINGLY, THE SALON HAD AVAILABILITY FOR A haircut anytime today. After his confrontation with Chloe on the sidewalk, he'd found Hook, Line, and Scissors and put on his game face. As frustrated as he was with Chloe, he would have to deal with that later. No one seemed to get under his skin like she did, but he couldn't let her derail this deal.

"What are you looking for today?" the woman asked him, after introducing herself as "Candi-with-an-i." She draped the cape around his shoulders and ran her fingers through his dark-brown locks.

He smiled at her in the mirror, turning on the charm. "Just freshen it up a bit. I like it short on the sides and longer on top. But things are a little grown out. Turns out I'm staying on the island a little longer than expected, so I figured I would get this taken care of while I am here. It seems like I am in capable hands," he added. A subtle compliment was never misplaced.

A slight blush rose in the older woman's cheeks. "Oh, you flatterer." She giggled, lifting her scissors and combing through his hair with a deft hand.

As she began to snip, Derrick glanced around the salon. It was small, cozy even, with a few chairs and bright floral decor. The smell of hairspray and shampoo mingled in the air.

"So," Candi started, "not many folks visit here in March. Here for business or pleasure?"

"Business," Derrick replied, debating how to keep things vague, but give enough detail to entice the woman to open up. "I'm just checking things out, you know. Evaluating some business opportunities."

Candi's eyes lit up with interest. "Oh, you're the one everyone's talking about! The local message board is all abuzz about this resort you want to build."

Derrick leaned forward slightly, trying to keep his tone casual. "Really? What have you heard?"

"Well, you know how small towns are," she began, her voice lowering conspiratorially. "Everyone knows everyone, and everyone has an opinion. I heard Jimmy wants you to get SICAB on board."

Derrick nodded. He was slightly surprised and concerned how much this random woman knew, but perhaps he shouldn't be. There was probably nothing else to talk about in this little town.

"Yes, that's right. What can you tell me about SICAB? Mr. DeBruin didn't get a chance to explain what kind of folks I'd be talking to." He flashed her a boyish smile. "My mom always told me to be prepared."

Candice pointed at his reflection in the mirror with her scissors. "Your momma was a smart woman. Let me see... where to start?"

She paused to gather her thoughts, trimming a lock of Derrick's hair and brushing the clippings off his cape. Derrick waited, trying to be patient but feeling a flicker of irritation as she seemed to take her sweet time.

"Well, there's Raymond, of course," she finally continued. "He owns the charter plane business. We all call him Rummy. Nice guy, but very protective of the island's way of life. Then there's Rick Bastida. He's a contractor, super successful. Lives here but works construction on the mainland. He's practical, straight-forward. Not much gets by him, but he would never do anything to jeopardize Sanctuary's way of life.

Derrick nodded, mentally cataloging each name and their potential influence.

"There's Officer Gibbons," Candi continued. "Alex is young, eager. Still trying to make a name for himself. Oh, and Paul Solheim, now there's an interesting one.

He used to work in construction but retired a few years ago. Comes from one of the founding families, so his opinion holds a lot of weight. His family is big on conservation. They even donated the land for Seven Pines in the 1950s. Then there's Stephen Warren, the fire chief. Tough but fair, you know the type."

Derrick made a note that Solheim might be a tough one. The tract of land they were looking at was currently completely undeveloped, except for a few hiking trails. The resort would definitely change the landscape.

Candi paused to adjust her grip on the scissors, her brow furrowing in concentration. Derrick watched her reflection in the mirror, noting the care she took with each snip. The warmth of the room and the rhythmic snipping of the scissors were almost soothing, but he remained focused on the information she was providing.

"Pastor Olsen from Prince of Peace church is also on the board," she went on. "He's all about community and kindness. And then there's Terry Camden, who happens to be my husband. He's got a good head on his shoulders, but of course, I'm a bit biased."

Derrick chuckled politely, encouraging her to continue.

"Let's see. We can't forget about Cathy. Have you been to Cathy's Cupcakes? I swear the woman is in her seventies but hasn't slowed down a bit. She's been on the island forever. Knows everyone and everything. I feel like I'm missing someone… Hmmm." She paused for a moment. "For the life of me, I can't remember who it is right now!" She laughed it off.

Derrick kept his tone light. "Sounds like quite the group. Do you think they'll have a problem with someone new on the island?"

Candi tilted her head, considering. "Well, they're a mix. Some are set in their ways, like Rummy and Cathy. But others, like Rick and Officer Gibbons, might be more open to new ideas. It's hard to say. They care about this island a lot, and they'll scrutinize anything that might change it."

Derrick nodded, absorbing her words. The group seemed to be made of businessmen and women that would understand the opportunity and the benefit of jobs on the island. He could speak their language, get them on his side. It all seemed manageable.

Candi's hands continued their work, deftly trimming and shaping his hair. The rhythmic snip of the scissors and the warm, homey atmosphere of the salon contrasted sharply with Derrick's calculating thoughts. He would have to tread carefully, ensuring that his project was seen as beneficial rather than disruptive.

"Thanks for the rundown, Candi," he said as she finished up. "You've been a big help."

She smiled warmly, brushing off the last of the clippings. "Anytime, hon. Good luck with your project."

Derrick paid for his haircut, tipping generously. As he stepped out of the salon and into the crisp island air, he smiled. He would win over SICAB, one way or another. The Family Adventure Resort was going to happen, and nothing would stand in his way. Or distract him.

A distraction like Chloe was exactly what he couldn't afford. Their history didn't matter. *Couldn't* matter.

He still couldn't believe she was here. After all these years, Chloe had been standing right in front of him this morning. How many times had he imagined what he'd say? How many times had he thought about having Sully track her down, just so he knew she was okay?

He could imagine the raised eyebrow he'd get from the unflappable private investigator he kept on retainer. The man's thoroughness had given him an edge in more negotiations than he could count. Derrick had never technically blackmailed anyone, but when you knew someone's secrets, you were playing with a stacked deck.

Multiple times over the past six years, he'd almost instructed Sully to find Chloe. It wasn't like she'd be hiding. But Derrick always talked himself out of it.

She knew where to find him if she changed her mind about them.

But why should she? She'd been right about him. He couldn't give her the kind of life she wanted. She was better off away from him. But why had she come to Sanctuary Island of all places? What kind of life could an award-winning chef build here?

He glanced around the quiet town square. It was a ghost town.

Derrick stepped inside the Eastside Cafe, checking his watch to confirm that Shaun would be here soon. His eyes slid to a woman standing at the counter, her back to him.

"Here you go, Chloe," the server said, handing her the drink. "I don't know how you can drink cold coffee on a cold day."

Chloe's laugh floated through the small cafe, and he felt his body buzz in response.

"Even if I order it hot, I forget about it while I'm cooking and end up drinking it cold anyway. Figure I might as well skip the scalding-my-tongue part." With a wave to the cashier, Chloe turned toward him. She stopped short, her eyes widening. For a second, he thought maybe they were red from crying, but that would be ridiculous. She was the one who left him.

"Chloe, I–"

She shook her head. "Nope." She lowered her eyes and headed for the door.

"Come on. You're going to have to talk–"

Her head snapped up. "You no longer get to tell me what to do, Derrick. You're on my turf now. And I don't have to do a thing if I don't want to." Her tone left no room for argument, but Derrick had never needed much anyway.

"You're always so unreasonable," he argued. If she would just talk to him, maybe they could get past this.

She balked, her steps pausing as she passed him. Finally, she was being–

Derrick's entire body froze in shock as the sharp edges of ice cubes and frigid streams of creamy coffee hit his face and dripped to the floor. His mouth fell open as he glanced down, watching tan rivulets drip down the collar of his wool coat and onto his shoes and the grungy tile floor.

He lifted his eyes to her face. Her mouth was open in an adorable O-shape, her eyes wide, as though she were as surprised as him at what had just happened. Slowly, her hand came to her mouth, covering it as he saw the beginning of a smile take over her features before she straightened, squaring her shoulders.

Had she seriously dumped her coffee on him? He blinked, his lashes wet and heavy.

"I can't believe you just did that." His voice held a

warning, laced with something that was almost a growl. It was a timbre that had easily cowed grown men in a boardroom.

Chloe tilted her chin up farther, refusing to back down. "Is this where you ask me if I know who you are? Because newsflash for you: I know exactly who you are, Derrick Lee Webster. And I want absolutely nothing to do with you."

With that, the short firecracker marched to the door. As she pushed through it, she called back, "Sorry about the mess, Winona. I'll make it up to you."

"Don't even worry about it," the server said with glee.

Derrick couldn't help but watch her retreating figure. That was twice that she'd walked away from him. And yet, he itched with the urge to chase after her.

seven

CHLOE

Chloe's heart raced as she nearly sprinted back to The Bluebell. Her face burned with humiliation and regret. Surely, this part had been a dream. Maybe she'd slipped on a patch of ice outside The Pearl and she was knocked out. Or there was something being sprayed in the park and she was hallucinating.

Because other than dreaming or absolute insanity, the only other option was that she had actually dumped a perfectly good iced coffee all over her ex-fiancé.

She groaned in realization. She'd just assaulted Derrick with an iced coffee. Technically, she was pretty sure that Officer Gibbons would be happy to take her word if she insisted that it had been an accident, if Derrick leaned into the evil villain role and decided to press charges.

And maybe worst of all, now she didn't even have the delicious cup of sugary caffeine to help her through the rest of this awful day. That had been a stupid, impulsive decision. But he'd just made her so angry! How dare he talk to her like he *knew* her. He didn't know her at all. And whatever he said, he didn't deserve a minute of her time.

When Chloe returned to The Bluebell, Marissa practically ran down the hallway toward the employee entrance to greet her. Trying to delay the inevitable, Chloe held up a hand.

"Give me a second, Mare. I've been walking around all morning and my feet are frozen."

Marissa huffed her disappointment. "Fine, but don't think you're getting away without telling me what happened this morning. It has to have something to do with that handsome billionaire, doesn't it? Ooh, did he wink at you? He winked at me when they were checking in yesterday and I thought my pacemaker was going to malfunction."

Chloe rolled her eyes at her boss's incessant, animated questions. "He's not a billionaire. And no, he didn't wink at me."

Marissa waved a hand. "Well, then what happened? I have never—in six years—seen you drop a plate. Or leave a dirty kitchen!"

Chloe opened the door to the kitchen, expecting it to be in the same chaotic state she left it, but the counters were cleared and wiped down.

She turned to Marissa. "You cleaned the kitchen?" Moisture gathered in her eyes at the realization. "You hate doing dishes," she continued, her voice rapidly disappearing into a whisper as the emotion overcame her. She didn't deserve this woman.

Marissa's arm curled around her shoulder. "That's true, I do. But I love you. And after you ran out of here today, the only thing I could think to do to help you was clean up the mess you left."

Chloe turned into the embrace and gave Marissa a hug, sniffing back her tears. "Well, you might as well come on in for some lunch and hear the whole story. Because if you thought this kitchen was messy, wait until I tell you about the time I almost got married."

Marissa's eyes widened and her mouth fell open. She was frozen for a moment, but then seemed to snap out of it. "Whoa. Okay. Let me just turn up the volume on the phone so I can hear it if it rings."

While Marissa ducked back to the reception desk, Chloe pulled off her coat and flicked her apron over her head, finding solace in the familiar movements. She pulled some meat and cheese from the fridge, raiding the supplies she'd purchased for the catering order that she now knew had been for Derrick. Now she wished she'd put extra olives on the tray, since he hated them so much.

Marissa bustled into the kitchen, eagerly pulling up a barstool to the corner of the stainless-steel counter. Over the years, this had become the spot where the two of them chatted the most, while Chloe prepped breakfast or evening reception. Over coffee in the mornings or lemonade in the afternoons, it was always a bright spot in her day.

She wasn't even sure why she hadn't told Marissa about her engagement to Derrick before now. It wasn't as if she still had feelings for him. Maybe part of her was ashamed that it had taken such a disastrous relationship for her to seek out the life she found here. That her faith had been so weak back then, it had been nearly nonexistent.

The people on this island, Marissa included, had healed her in a way she hadn't really even known she needed. She had been hurt by Derrick, for sure. But she was broken beyond that. And it had taken being in a place where people cared for her, saw her vulnerability, and didn't judge her for it, for her to truly find peace.

"So, are you gonna start at the beginning, or do I have to guess?"

Chloe gave a small smile. "Let me tell you a story

about an up-and-coming chef who falls for the tall, dark, and handsome businessman." Chloe quickly regaled the origins of her relationship with Derrick Webster. Yes, that Derrick Webster, the heir to Webster Hotels.

"In the end, though, he chose work over our relationship too many times for me to be comfortable promising to spend forever with him." She hadn't been enough to make him happy. And it had taken a really long time to realize that maybe that hadn't been her fault. It had taken fully accepting Jesus again to understand that Derrick's choices were his own.

But that didn't make them hurt her any less. A woman wanted nothing more than her partner to be so overwhelmed with love for her that he would sacrifice everything else. To be treasured enough. And he hadn't loved her like that.

Marissa's eyes hadn't left Chloe's during the entire story, even as she fumbled for cheese and crackers on the lunch tray.

"And now he just showed up here? Are you kidding me? This is like *Dawson's Creek* or something."

Chloe buried her face in her hands. "I walked into breakfast this morning and I saw him and I panicked. I'm so sorry I left you in a lurch, but I just... I couldn't face him." She shook her head, glancing back up at her boss, mentor, and friend. "A fact I confirmed when I dumped my coffee on him at Eastside." Marissa gasped and Chloe groaned. "Why does he have to be here?"

Everything was finally going well in her life. She had friends. She had a job she loved. Her faith was strong and she had a sense of contentment she'd been missing her whole life. How could she explain how much Derrick had hurt her?

"I've never been as heartbroken as I was when I realized that Derrick would never give me his whole heart. I left his ring on the counter with a note, and I took off. I landed here, of all places. And seriously, I've never been happier."

Marissa smiled. "You belonged here the instant you stepped foot off the ferry."

Chloe nodded. "Exactly. And now he's going to try to ruin it!" The thought of Derrick interfering in Sanctuary made her blood boil again. She thought back to what she'd heard from Rummy and Paul at the restaurant last night.

That made Marissa frown. "What do you mean?"

Chloe made a face. "His big, stupid resort plan. He's got some grand idea that he's going to *save the island.*" She sat up straight and wobbled side to side, impersonating the man himself with a giant stick up his rear, lowering her voice.

Marissa laughed. "I didn't realize we needed saving."

"Exactly what I said! But he's so arrogant, I'm sure he assumes that whatever plan he came up with must be the greatest idea known to man. And he's got the money and the connections to make it happen. Or"—her lips twisted into a wry smile—"he thinks he does. But he underestimates me and my place on this island."

"Uh-oh." Marissa's voice was cautious. "What are you thinking?"

Chloe gave a mischievous grin. "I'm just saying that he might find the town a little less accommodating than he anticipates."

Marissa gave her a warning look.

Chloe held up her hands. "Nothing awful. And nothing that would look bad for the inn, I promise."

Marissa sighed. "Are you sure, Chloe? The last thing we need is some upset billionaire ticked off at us. It's hard enough as it is."

Chloe immediately stiffened, a frown crossing her lips. "What do you mean?"

Marissa waved her hands, as though she could wave away Chloe's concern. Not happening. "It's nothing major, but you know things are always tight. The busy season gets us through, but winters are lean. And it's fine," she emphasized. "But if Webster Hotels were to try to take us out? The Bluebell would be a smear on the bottom of his well-polished shoes."

Chloe laid a hand on Marissa's forearm. "I won't let

that happen, okay, Mare?" She meant every word. The only thing more important than kicking Derrick out of Sanctuary was protecting Marissa and The Bluebell. As it turned out, those were basically one and the same. So that was convenient.

eight

DERRICK

THE BELLS ABOVE THE DOOR RANG AS SHAUN WALKED through the cafe door Chloe had just walked out. His eyes widened when he saw Derrick standing in the middle of the restaurant. Derrick supposed he made quite a picture, dripping with coffee and frozen in place.

"Whoa, boss. What–"

"Don't ask," Derrick said sharply, pulling a pile of napkins from the metal dispenser on the nearest table. "Just… don't ask." He mopped his face and chest as best as he could, trying not to wince at the small pieces of paper that stuck to his wool coat as the napkin disintegrated.

It was obvious that curiosity was killing him, but Shaun didn't press. "Okayyy then. Shall we?" He gestured to a table and they both sat. “This place is unbelievable, D.”

Derrick tried not to frown at the nickname, but Shaun didn’t even notice as he continued.

"Did you know that only seven hundred people live here during the winter? Or that during the off-season, The Lantern Room restaurant is only open once a week? Oh, and the Shore View Palace.” Shaun whistled. “I have some good stuff about the Shore View.”

Derrick’s curiosity was piqued, but he didn’t need small-town gossip. “Stuff that’s going to help us build a Family Adventure Resort?”

Shaun’s smile grew. “I think so.”

"Okay, well, hold that thought. My haircut was quite fruitful as well.”

Shaun’s eyes flicked up to Derrick’s hair. “Looks pretty good, I guess. And I bet it didn’t cost two hundred bucks, either.”

Derrick ran a hand over the back of his head. He’d felt a bit ridiculous when he realized that Candi had given him pretty much an identical style to his normal barber but charged a tenth of the price. He’d tipped her generously to make up for it, and to thank her for the scoop on SICAB.

"Yes, well. You were one hundred percent right, that woman talked my ear off the entire haircut. Once I asked about the advisory board, she practically gave me the life story of every single member."

Shaun nodded and his smile spread. "Awesome. What's the story?"

"Nothing we can't handle. Typical stuff—older guys who have retired or still own a business on the island. Couple of construction guys, someone who works in Public Works. Nobody that I would view as inherently hostile to us." Derrick had been afraid someone from the Palace resort would be on the committee, but apparently it was owned by a specialty corporate chain and the owners were pretty hands-off.

"Oh, speaking of the Palace. Let me tell you what I found."

Derrick pointed at the counter where the menu was posted. "Can we order first? I'm starving."

They ordered at the counter and came back with a small plastic number to display on their table, despite being one of only two tables filled.

"Okay, go ahead." Derrick waved a hand to Shaun.

Shaun shifted in his seat, the anticipation rising on his face. "Okay, get this. The Shore View Palace is no longer owned by the Hallgren family, but when they sold it, part of the deal was that the corporation use the same contracts with vendors as they had before."

Derrick nodded as he processed the information.

"So they didn't want the corporation to cut out all the local vendors?"

"Kind of. But they also have a few... particular clauses in their vendor contracts that are most unusual."

Derrick narrowed his eyes as Shaun paused, his flair for the dramatic taking over as he waited to build suspense.

"If you're unmarried over the age of thirty, you can't be a vendor or employee."

Derrick's eyes flew open. "What?"

"I know," Shaun added with glee. "Isn't that the craziest thing you've ever heard?"

Derrick sat in stunned silence for a moment. "I can't believe the corporation agreed to that."

"Right? This guy named Curtis said that the company probably thought they could redo the contracts a few years later, but apparently someone from the Hallgren family is some sort of legal wizard, because the purchase agreement and the contract are absolutely binding and legal. There's nothing they can do."

Derrick hummed in consideration. "Don't get me wrong, this is super unorthodox and really strange. But how does this help us?"

Shaun shrugged. "I haven't figured that out yet. But surely there are disgruntled former employees or people who haven't been hired because of this craziness. We could sell ourselves as an equal-opportunity employer and all that."

"Okay, okay, I see where you're going with this. Let's table it for now and see what makes sense as we build out our argument. Our meeting is next Tuesday with SICAB. Tomorrow, I want to visit the site with Mr. Beekman and put a little pressure on him. I'll feel better talking to SICAB if we have a firm commitment from him. Plus, I want to spend some more time at the site. It looks perfect on paper, but you know how I like to get a feel for it and make sure all the views are perfect."

"Sounds good, boss. I've got the blueprints in my room. Do you want them at the meeting?"

Derrick hesitated, considering. "Not yet."

The server brought over their food, steaming plates filled with fries and burgers with toppings oozing from the sides. The scent made Derrick's mouth water. Whatever hesitation he had at a restaurant that made you stand and order at the counter, paying before you received your food, was quickly replaced with appreciation at the feast in front of him. The sight of the juicy burgers and the crispy, golden fries was a welcome distraction.

Derrick took a bite of his burger, the savory flavors exploding in his mouth. The tang of the special sauce mingled perfectly with the juicy beef and crisp lettuce.

He chewed thoughtfully, savoring the taste before speaking.

"Alright, let's outline our next steps," Derrick said, wiping his mouth with a napkin. "First, we need to solidify our pitch to SICAB. I want to highlight the benefits our Family Adventure Resort will bring to the island."

Shaun nodded, his mouth full of fries. "Jobs, tourism, increased revenue for local businesses." He gestured with a fry to emphasize each point.

"Exactly. We should also emphasize our commitment to preserving the island's natural beauty. Sounds like some of the board members are pretty conservation-minded."

"Good catch," Shaun said. "We can do a detailed environmental impact study to show that we can develop the resort without harming the ecosystem."

"Perfect."

Shaun swallowed and leaned forward, his expression serious. "What about community support? We need to get the locals on our side. If they back us, SICAB will have a harder time saying no."

Derrick took a sip of his soda, the cold bubbles refreshing his palate. "I've been thinking about that. We should host a town hall meeting. Lay out our plans, answer questions, address concerns. Show them we're invested in the community, not just looking to exploit it."

"I like it," Shaun said, reaching for another fry. "We could also partner with some local businesses for the event. Maybe have food from Cathy's Cupcakes. Make it a community event."

"Agreed," Derrick said, nodding. "And while we're at it, we should try to have one-on-one meetings with other key community members. Get a feel for their concerns and see how we can address them proactively."

Shaun wiped his hands on a napkin and pulled out his phone. "I'll start drafting a list of people we need to talk to. Sounds like maybe that Solheim guy is probably a good call."

Derrick interrupted, raising a hand. "Don't forget there's a new member, too. Candi mentioned it, but she couldn't remember who it was."

"Right," Shaun said, tapping at his screen. "I'll dig into that and see if I can find out who it is. Better to know who we're dealing with."

The two men continued to strategize, the conversation flowing as easily as the scent of the delicious food around them. Derrick's mind was already racing ahead, envisioning the resort, the benefits it would bring, and the challenges they would overcome. Everything depended on this resort being approved. Derrick trusted his gut, and it told him that Family Adventure Resorts was the next big market for Webster Hotels. These resorts were going to take Webster to the next level, with him at the helm.

The board wouldn't be able to argue with success like that. And the vultures trying to steal his father's legacy from him wouldn't have a leg to stand on. Family Adventure Resorts were the key to the future of Webster Hotels. And Sanctuary Island was the key to Family Adventure Resorts. As much as he hated to admit it when the market research team came with their location strategies. It was the perfect fit.

As long as SICAB approved.

By the time they finished their meal, Derrick felt a renewed sense of determination. He glanced at Shaun, who was busily typing notes into his phone. "Alright, let's get to work. We have a lot to do before the meeting next week."

Shaun looked up, his eyes gleaming with excitement. "I'm on it, boss. This island won't know what hit it."

As they left the diner, the bell above the door jingled softly. The midday sun glared off the snow covering the quaint streets of Sanctuary Island. Derrick took a deep breath, the crisp, cool air filling his lungs. Despite it still being winter, there was a hint of spring in the sunshine.

Amidst his growing confidence, thoughts of Chloe

flickered in his mind. Her fiery resistance to his presence, the passion in her eyes—it both frustrated and intrigued him. Why would she possibly care so much about Sanctuary?

She somehow seemed like exactly the same woman he'd thought he loved all those years ago. And yet... she was also different. Was it simply because she hated him now? Or was there something more to her transformation?

nine

CHLOE

Chloe moved around the kitchen of The Hummingbird and Bluebell Inn with practiced ease. The aroma of freshly baked bread and spiced apples for the next day's stuffed french toast breakfast filled the air. She meticulously arranged a platter of delicate smoked salmon canapés and bite-sized caprese skewers with cherry tomatoes and mozzarella. Each piece was placed with care, ensuring a balance of colors and flavors that would appeal to the guests at the evening reception. Even if she sort of wanted Derrick to choke on a cherry tomato, the last thing he tasted would be delicious.

She carried the platter into the dining room. The soft, shaded sunlight filtered through the windows, subtly gleaming on the polished wood of the side table and cabinets, casting a warm and inviting ambiance over the dining room. A fire crackled in the hearth and soft music played in the background. The Bluebell really was a lovely little place.

She placed a bowl of herbed olives on the table next to the other appetizers. Derrick wouldn't eat them, but she was pretending she didn't know him.

If only that were true.

The dining room door swung open behind her. Chloe turned, expecting one of the staff, but her breath caught when she saw Derrick standing in the doorway.

His presence was imposing, even in the stately dining room. He looked slightly disheveled, with his dark hair a bit tousled from the wind. For a moment, they just stared at each other, the air thick with unspoken words and lingering tension.

"Evening reception doesn't start for twenty more minutes," Chloe stated, her voice sharper than her favorite chef's knife. She clutched a small pair of tongs as though she were ready to fight off a wild animal with them.

"I was looking for you," Derrick replied, stepping farther into the room and letting the door close behind him. "I thought we could talk."

She tried to ignore the feeling of being trapped in the room as the door closed. "Talk?" Chloe echoed, a bitter laugh escaping her lips. "About what? Your plans to ruin everything I love about this place?"

Derrick's jaw tightened. "It's not like that, Chloe. I'm trying to help this island. Create jobs, bring in more tourists—"

"Destroy its soul," she interrupted, setting the tongs down on a white porcelain plate with a clatter. "You don't understand this place like I do."

They stood in silence, the only sound the gentle hum of the radiator and the soft clinking of ice falling into the kitchen's freezer. Chloe busied herself pointlessly rearranging the olives, trying to ignore the way Derrick's presence seemed to fill the room.

"I remember when you made these for my aunt and uncle's anniversary," Derrick said suddenly, nodding toward the olives. His voice was softer, tinged with nostalgia. "You spent hours perfecting the recipe."

Chloe paused, the memory flooding back. It had been a warm summer evening, the two of them working side by side in a tiny kitchen, laughing and teasing each other as they cooked. The way he had looked at her then, with such genuine affection and admiration, had made her heart flutter.

She glanced up at him, her anger momentarily forgotten. "Your uncle said they were the best olives he'd ever had," she said quietly, a small smile playing on her lips despite herself. With the hurt and pain of the end of their relationship, it was easier to forget that there had been good times as well.

Derrick's eyes softened. "He still talks about them, you know. Every time we have a family gathering, he asks if I can get the recipe from you."

Chloe's heart ached at the shared memory, a bittersweet reminder of what they once had. "Those were good times," she admitted, her voice barely above a whisper.

Derrick took a step closer, his eyes searching hers. "They were," he agreed. "We had a lot of good times, Chloe."

For a moment, the animosity between them seemed to fade, replaced by the warmth of old memories. Chloe shook her head, stepping back and putting the counter between them.

"But that was a long time ago," she said, her tone firm once more. "Things are different now. We're not friends, Derrick." For every good memory where they'd spent time together, there were half a dozen others. Waiting in restaurants when he never showed, attending a ballet alone when a meeting ran late, making excuses when he missed the dinner party they were supposed to host *together.*

Derrick's expression hardened, the brief connection slipping away. "They don't have to be," he said, a hint of frustration in his voice. "We were a good team once."

Chloe sighed, the weight of their shared past and uncertain future pressing down on her. "You know what I realized? That day when you chose to go to Omaha instead of flying with me to Maine? Like so many times before, you chose work over me. I realized that we were never a team. Not really." She pressed her lips together, pushing back the emotion again. "You've always been Team Derrick. And there's no room for anyone else on that team."

"That's not true," he argued.

Chloe threw up her hands. "You want to change everything about this place, and I want to preserve it. We're on opposite sides."

He opened his mouth to argue more, but before he could speak, the door swung open again, and Marissa bustled in.

"Oh, sorry," she said, stopping short when she saw Derrick. "I didn't mean to interrupt."

Chloe forced a smile. "It's fine, Marissa. We were just finishing up."

Shaun stepped halfway into the room, his phone to his ear, covering the mouthpiece with one hand. He found Derrick. "Boss, it's Julie. She needs to know about the Harvest of Hope Gala. Your plus one?"

Derrick's jaw clenched, his eyes lingering on Chloe for a moment longer before he turned to leave. "We'll talk more later," he said, his tone making it clear it wasn't a suggestion. He followed Shaun out the door, speaking in low whispers she couldn't understand.

Chloe watched him go, her heart heavy with conflicting emotions—the most unsettling being the discomfort she felt at the idea of his plus one at the gala. Harvest of Hope had been one of her favorite charities when she lived in Chicago. The program provided meals for at-risk kids all across the city. They'd attended the gala together several times. It shouldn't be surprising that he'd have someone else on his arm at those events now.

Marissa gave her a questioning look, but Chloe shook her head, not ready to discuss it. Instead, she focused on re-arranging the hors d'oeuvres, even though they were already perfect, the familiar routine bringing her a measure of comfort. Chloe took a deep breath, pushing thoughts of Derrick to the back of her mind. She had a job to do, and she wasn't about to let him derail her focus.

But as she finished the preparation for tomorrow morning, she couldn't entirely banish the memory of their conversation—or the lingering ache it left behind. Her thoughts kept drifting back to Derrick, to the way his eyes had softened when he mentioned the olives, to the shared memories that still had the power to connect them, even after all this time.

She walked home as the sun set, and once inside her small home, Chloe found herself standing by the window, staring out at the rapidly melting snow. She wrapped her arms around herself, feeling the chill seep in.

She thought about Derrick's determination, his resort, and the way it clashed so fiercely with her own desires for the island. But she also remembered the good times, the love they'd shared, and the way he had once made her feel like anything was possible. How deeply he'd hurt her with his apathy. She couldn't let herself linger on those good memories. She had to remind herself of the times he'd let her down. That was what Derrick had always done and what he would always do.

But she also couldn't ignore the reality of their opposing goals. She loved this place with all her heart, and she would fight to preserve it, no matter what.

And if that meant standing against Derrick, then so be it. The island—and the life she had built here—came before whatever shared history they might have.

ten

DERRICK

After much deliberation on the best way to navigate the island with cars not allowed in town, Derrick and Shaun borrowed bicycles from The Hummingbird and Bluebell to take to the hopeful site of the Family Adventure Resort. The sunshine from yesterday had melted the last of the snow on the streets, though it still lingered in the shade and on the grass.

As they rode, the crisp early-spring air greeted them, carrying with it the scent of pine from the woods that covered most of the island. When they stopped at the small parking area, a pebbled beach stretched out before them.

Near the shore, the frozen water shimmered in the morning sunlight, while farther out across Lake Huron, dark waters rolled in the wind. Across the road from the public parking, the dense forest stood silent and watchful. A well-worn trailhead marked with 'Private Property' indicated that tourists frequently ignored the posted signs and hiked through these woods anyway.

A quick glance around showed no sign of Mr. Beekman. Derrick glanced at his watch, frowning at the delay. It was already five minutes after the hour. He turned to the beach, scanning the shoreline. His eyes paused at the sight of someone huddled in a blanket, blond hair blowing in the breeze. The exact color of—

Shaun called his name, but Derrick was already several strides toward the beach down the short boardwalk.

Was it her?

As he approached, her profile came into focus. Derrick took in her silhouette against the backdrop of the frozen shoreline. She seemed lost in thought, her expression distant. Almost troubled. She held her knees to her chest, staring over them to the lake.

"Chloe," he called out softly, his voice carrying over the gentle lapping of the waves.

She turned to face him, her eyes guarded but curious. "Derrick," she replied, her voice tinged with resignation. "Of course you'd be here."

There was a pause, the air heavy with unspoken words and unresolved tension. She was perched on an outcropping of larger rocks protruding from the smaller pebbled beach.

"I didn't expect to see you here," Derrick ventured, taking a few hesitant steps closer to her. Chloe remained where she was, her posture stiff but her gaze steady.

"I like to come here to think," she admitted, her voice barely above a whisper. "And today, I have a lot to think about."

Derrick nodded, understanding the weight of her words. He sat down next to her, and she scooted over slightly to make room. They sat in silence for a moment, the only sound the soft crunch of stones shifting beneath their feet.

"I know we're on opposite sides of this," Derrick began, choosing his words carefully, "but I want you to know that I respect your passion for this island."

Chloe regarded him warily, her expression guarded yet tinged with a glimmer of surprise. "And I respect your ambition," she replied, her voice softening slightly. "But that doesn't change the fact that I believe your resort would change this place forever."

Derrick sighed, running a hand through his hair in frustration. "It will," he admitted. "But I also believe it could bring much-needed jobs and opportunities to the people here. And change doesn't always have to be bad."

If there was one thing he'd learned from years in

business, it was that change was the requisite predecessor to progress.

Their conversation was interrupted by a holler from the direction of the parking lot. Derrick looked back and saw Travis and Shaun quickly approaching Chloe's solitary hideout.

Derrick had been frustrated with Travis's tardiness, but now he was even more disappointed that his conversation with Chloe had been cut short. He stood and greeted Travis with a forced smile, hiding his annoyance beneath a veneer of professionalism.

"Mr. Beekman," Derrick said, his tone polite yet tinged with impatience. "I was starting to wonder if you'd forgotten about our meeting."

Travis shrugged nonchalantly, a sheepish grin playing on his lips. "Sorry about that. Got held up with some business matters," he replied. Despite his words, his voice was entirely unrepentant.

Derrick raised an eyebrow, a flicker of suspicion in his mind. He knew Travis was in financial trouble, and the man seemed a bit too slick.

"Have you had the property line surveyed?" Derrick asked.

"Oh, absolutely. This little parking lot sits pretty much dead center. Quarter mile that way," he pointed to the west, "and a quarter mile that way." He pointed to the east.

"Property starts at the road and extends about a half mile back. You're lookin' at one-hundred-and-sixty acres that have been in my family for a hundred and fifty years."

Derrick absorbed the information. Most resorts needed less than ten acres to have room for pools and other amenities. But his resort needed extra room for a snow-tubing run, cross-country skiing trails, snow-mobile rentals, in addition to a large indoor pool space. One-sixty would be more than enough for all that plus private hiking trails.

As they talked, Derrick walked the line of unease that lingered between them, a silent tugging of the delicate balance of power that existed between buyer and seller. He noticed Chloe's gaze occasionally drifting toward the horizon, her brows furrowed in deep thought, and he couldn't help but wonder what was going through her mind.

In retrospect, he should have moved the conversation away from where she could eavesdrop, but it was a bit late for that. He hadn't wanted to walk away from her, he realized.

Travis continued to discuss the details of the land sale casually, but his eyes were slightly wide with an obvious desire to make the sale. Derrick listened attentively, nodding at all the right moments, but his mind was elsewhere, preoccupied with thoughts of the impact his resort would have on the island and its inhabitants.

It was obvious that Travis was pushing to sell, despite how casual he was attempting to be about the whole thing. Perhaps he could assure the town that having Webster Hotels come in would be preferable to some large condominium developer who would build towering condo buildings. At least his Family Adventure Resort would carry the same old-fashioned, rustic charm of the island.

Ideas whirled in his mind. Perhaps with this much land, they could expand the footprint and cap the height of the hotel at three stories high. Then, it wouldn't detract from the natural landscape when you were looking from other parts of the island.

Eventually, Travis gave Derrick the verbal confirmation he needed, assuring him that, as long as SICAB and the mayor were on board, he would sell the land. Derrick thanked him, masking his relief behind a mask of professionalism.

"That's great to hear, Travis. I appreciate your cooperation."

Travis grinned, seemingly pleased to have reached an agreement. "No problem, Mr. Webster. Let me know when you're ready to move forward, and we can get the paperwork sorted out."

They shook hands, and Shaun offered to walk Travis back up to the parking lot.

Once Travis was out of earshot, Derrick turned back to Chloe, his expression softening as he regarded her. "Well, that went better than expected," he remarked, attempting to break the tension that still hung in the air between them.

Chloe offered him a tight-lipped smile, her eyes betraying a hint of skepticism. "It seems like you got what you wanted," she replied, her tone guarded.

Derrick nodded, choosing his words carefully. "True, but it's not just about what I want. I genuinely believe that this resort could be good for Sanctuary."

Chloe's expression softened slightly, her gaze meeting his with resignation and understanding. "I know you believe that," she said softly, "but you also don't actually know what would be good for us at all. You've been here for twenty-four hours, Derrick.

Derrick sighed, running a hand through his hair in frustration. He knew Chloe's concerns were valid, but he couldn't let them deter him from pursuing his vision. "Fine. Then show me," he said earnestly. "Show me what is so special about this little town with nothing going on seven months out of the year."

It was quite possible he'd just lost his mind, because the last thing he had time for was Chloe dragging him around town and trying to convince him to change his mind. There was no way she could do it anyway. There was too much riding on this with his Board of Directors.

Chloe regarded him silently for a moment, her expression unreadable. Derrick couldn't help but feel a pang of regret at the distance that remained between them. Why was he so eager to be on friendly terms with the woman who had abandoned him and their future together?

"It's been twenty years since I've been here. I know why I loved it back then," he admitted quietly, careful to check that Shaun was out of ear shot. "Show me why you love it now?"

Chloe pressed her lips together. "You'll think about building your resort somewhere else?"

The idea filled him with a surprising pang of sadness. He knew in his gut that Sanctuary Island was the perfect spot. And the research from his marketing team backed him up. But he nodded. "Yes, I'll find out what you love so much, and I'll carefully consider our plans."

As they stood there on the windswept beach, surrounded by the beauty of nature and the weight of their conflicting desires, Derrick couldn't help but wonder if there would ever be a way for them to bridge the divide that had grown between them. But for now, all he could do was focus on the task at hand and hope that, in time, they would find a way to reconcile their differences for the greater good of Sanctuary Island.

Her eyes slid out to the water beyond the shoreline. “Okay,” she said. “I’m in. Be at the community center tonight at seven.”

“I’ll be there,” he promised.

eleven

CHLOE

Chloe finished her work at The Hummingbird and Bluebell Inn earlier than usual. After serving breakfast, she'd taken her walk on the beach. When she got back, she quickly prepared the evening reception and left Marissa directions for setting it out.

The conversation with Derrick and Travis lingered in her mind, and while she'd agreed to show Derrick the best side of the island off-season, she also wasn't going to sit on her pockets and wait for the meeting next week without doing everything she could to stop Derrick. She'd stayed up way too late the other night, and the special ordered signs would arrive via two-day air courtesy of the daily supply flight that brought the mail during the winter while the ferry was closed.

The upcoming SICAB meeting was crucial to sending Derrick packing, and she needed to ensure that the community was aware of the proposed resort and its potential impact. Hence the twenty-five full-color signs she'd paid an arm and a leg to have ordered so quickly. Determined to rally support, today she planned to visit the local businesses and gather allies to her cause.

Before she left, she checked her email on the computer at Marissa's desk. Nothing new, she realized with a small frown. Absently, she clicked into her Junk folder. She usually checked her messages from her phone and forgot about it.

She scrolled past the usual scam messages, until a message from Raven Foods caught her eye. Chloe clicked in and read it quickly, excitement filling her. It was exactly the kind of partnership she'd been dreaming about for @ChloeIntheKitchen, her social media accounts. Fiona Raven was basically her celebrity chef idol. The woman was barely thirty-five but had her own daytime talk show, cooking show, line of high-quality frozen food, and was the headline host of the WBC Holiday Cooking Specials. Hashtag goals, seriously.

According to this email, Raven Foods wanted her to be part of a group of cooking influencers to do a behind-the-scenes campaign at Raven Foods manufacturing locations. It was an amazing opportunity.

Her eyes flicked back up to the date. They'd sent it two weeks ago?

Sugar.

Hurriedly, she pulled out her phone and dialed the contact number given.

"This is Gabbi Schmidt," came the voice when the ringing stopped.

Chloe took a deep breath. "Hi, Ms. Schmidt. This is Chloe Bennet, from @ChloeintheKitchen. I'm calling because I just now saw your invitation to the Raven Foods Factory to Fork campaign, and I am desperately hoping that I am not too late to take part."

Chloe was practically begging, but she didn't care. She was kicking herself for not seeing the email sooner. If she didn't get the opportunity, it would serve her right for dropping the ball on this.

"Oh, Miss Bennet, I'm glad you called. I was really disappointed we hadn't heard back from you. Fiona and I love your videos."

Chloe sat up straighter, heat rising in her cheeks as the compliment flooded her with the giddiness of a teen girl who'd just found out her crush liked her back. Did she really mean… Fiona? Like, Fiona Raven? "Wow, that's such an honor, ma'am."

"Uh-uh, none of that ma'am stuff."

Chloe giggled at the attitude and personality obvious in the woman she was talking to.

"Here's the deal, Chloe. I'm happy to let you keep your spot, but you might be pushing it to make it happen. The tour is in two days."

Chloe's heart sank. If she'd lived in Chicago, it would have been no big deal. But two days wasn't nearly enough time. Not from Sanctuary. Unless it was during the summer, she'd have to book a charter flight to the mainland, and then coordinate that with a flight out of Havensport. And there weren't that many flights out of Havensport.

"Oh, I understand." She sighed. "I'm afraid I won't be able to make that happen."

"Bummer," Gabbi said dramatically. "Tell you what. I'll send you the information, and if you can make it, then we'll see you there. And if not, we'll get you the next time around. Okay?"

Chloe agreed, but her heart wasn't in it. If she had just known earlier, maybe she could have made it work, but there was no chance. Darn this secluded island and the travel hoops they had to jump through.

"I hope I get to meet you in Chicago in a few days, Chloe! I know Fiona would, too."

Chloe winced. Knowing that it was in Chicago made it that much harder, because that would have been actually really doable with two weeks' notice.

"Thanks for the opportunity, Ms. Schmidt. I'll be in touch."

As Chloe stepped outside, the sun greeted her. The streets ran wet with the snow melt as the sun warmed the ground. It finally felt like winter was drawing to a close. Of course, the long-term forecast hinted at another storm in two-weeks, but she was choosing to be optimistic. Even with the bad news about the potential Raven Foods partnership, she knew how much someone's attitude affected everything else.

And she was on a mission. No matter what happened with her social media accounts, she still had something to accomplish here.

The streets were quiet, with only a few people out. As she reached the town square, she waved to Elijah, hobbling across the street in a short sleeve shirt. After a long winter, a sunny day with no wind felt like a heat wave. Chloe slipped off her coat, folded it over her arm, and headed toward her first stop: Whimsical Pages Bookstore.

The bell above the door jingled as she entered the cozy shop. Shelves of books lined the walls, and the cramped spaces twisted through the old house-turned-shop, winding from room to room of the store. Chloe knew from experience that a girl could get lost browsing for hours here. Guy Williams, the owner, looked up from behind the counter and greeted her with a friendly smile.

"Morning, Chloe! What brings you in?" He held up a

finger. "Oh, I have a new release from that author you like!"

"Really? I didn't realize Kari Trumbo had a new one out!" Chloe scurried to the desk, jokingly holding out grabby hands like an impatient toddler waiting for their favorite toy.

Guy shrugged. "I tucked it in the back for you. Give me a minute."

Chloe opened her mouth to reply, but Guy had already disappeared to the storeroom. When he returned a moment later, he handed her a thick book with a cowboy on the cover. Chloe immediately wanted to turn it over and read the back but resisted the urge.

"Thanks so much. I really love that you know what I like and go out of your way to save them for me."

Guy flashed a broad smile. "Of course, Chloe. That kind of thing is why we live in a place like this, despite the craziness of the season. Not that I'm complaining. Those vacation readers are voracious!"

Chloe laughed, knowing it was true. Some of them even read their book at breakfast at The Bluebell.

"That's kind of why I came to talk to you, actually. What have you heard about the SICAB meeting next week or this developer who is in town?"

Guy shook his head. "You know me. I stay off the rumor train. Why do you ask?"

Chloe explained what Derrick had in mind for the

resort and all the reasons she thought it would hurt the town. "It really seems like these people are going to come to the island during the winter and never leave the safety of his little resort. We'll have more air traffic and visitors doing irresponsible things in the snow and ice. He'll build his own restaurants in the resort, and that will even steal business from our local places during the season, not to mention the impact on our current hotels and inns."

She took a moment to catch her breath after the rant. "I think it's important that the community voices their concerns."

"You bring up some good points. I'm not too thrilled with the idea of a big resort coming in and changing the character of our town."

"Exactly," Chloe said, nodding. "Here's the deal. I've got some signs ordered. They should be here tomorrow, and I'm passing them out to any businesses who want to display them and show the mayor and the members of SICAB that they're opposed to the resort. Would you be willing to put one up in your window?"

"Absolutely," Guy agreed without hesitation. "Anything to protect Sanctuary."

"Thanks, Guy. I knew I could count on you." Chloe felt a sense of relief wash over her. She knew that Guy's support would encourage others to join the cause.

Next, she headed to the outskirts of town to Elijah's

mechanic garage. The smell of motor oil and the sound of clanging metal filled the air as she walked in. Elijah was working under the hood of a car, his hands covered in grease. He straightened up when he saw her and wiped his hands on a rag.

"Hey, Chloe. What can I do for you? Did you get a car I don't know about?"

Chloe smiled. "Hah, no. Who needs a car around here? I actually wanted to talk to you about this resort proposal. Have you heard anything?"

After a similar conversation as she had with Guy, she wrapped up with the same pitch. "I'm asking local businesses to display signs showing their opposition. I'll bring some around tomorrow. Would you be interested?"

"Count me in," Elijah said, nodding. "This island's been good to me. I'd hate to see it change for the worse."

Chloe thanked him and made her way to her next stop. Hook, Line & Scissors was pretty much the only place in town to get a haircut, and Candi was guaranteed to be the one with the most accurate information about anyone and everyone in Sanctuary. The salon wasn't busy, but the hum of a hairdryer and Candi's distinctive chatter filled the air. Candi was at her station, drying Gretta's hair while practically yelling to be heard over the dryer. She spotted Chloe and waved her over as she flipped off the blow-dryer and the shop grew blessedly quiet.

"Chloe! To what do I owe the pleasure? Is it about that handsome mainlander who came in here the other day? Tony said you two were looking pretty cozy over on Pebble Beach the other morning." Candi wiggled her eyebrows suggestively.

Chloe chose to ignore her attempt to get more information to spread around town. "Look, I know you know about the resort. Next week, SICAB is going to hear Derrick's proposal, and I want to make sure the community knows what's at stake."

"Oh, it's Derrick, is it?" Candi asked.

"Sounds awful familiar, if you ask me," said Gretta. She worked as the manager of the Shore View Palace and was currently watching the conversation in the mirror, absently flipping through a magazine.

Chloe bit back her frustration. Snapping back that no one had, in fact, asked for Gretta's opinion wouldn't be helpful.

"Come on, ladies. Gretta," she appealed to the hotelier, "you have to agree that some corporate indoor waterpark resort isn't what this island needs, right?"

Gretta tipped her head back and forth in indecision. "It would definitely make our winters even slower at the Palace. We already have to run a special once a month during the off-season to bring people in just to keep the doors open. And they'd compete with us during the summer, too."

Chloe nodded, then turned to Candi. "What about you?"

Candi pursed her lips. "I don't know, sugar. I kind of liked chatting with that handsome fellow. Liked what he had to say about more jobs and more visitors. Can you just imagine? What if we had enough visitors to keep Cathy's open more days during the season? It feels like the only time I'm craving a cupcake is when that blasted shop is closed. I hear that's what it's like on the mainland at that chicken restaurant. Closed on Sundays."

Chloe blinked back her amazement at Candi's ability to prattle on about absolutely nothing.

"I wish we could have cupcakes every day, too," she offered as an olive branch. She sighed. "What is it everyone is always saying? *We're not Mackinac Island,*" she quoted. "And you know as well as I do that we don't want to be."

Gretta chimed in with "Amen," which made Chloe smile.

Chloe continued, "But the way I see it, Webster Hotels is going to try to have everything people could possibly want in their resort, and guests would barely even venture out to the rest of the island. They'll be too busy bowling or swimming or snow tubing."

"Snow tubing?" Gretta asked, obviously dismayed at the idea. The Shore View Palace was a sprawling historic hotel with exacting standards and high-class finishes. And Gretta ran the place with a perfectly-shined silver fist.

Chloe didn't know how to get this conversation back on track. "I've got some signs about the issue arriving tomorrow. Can I bring one for your window?" she asked Candi.

"I like what you're doing, but I think I'm gonna stay out of this one. Look, with my Terry on the board anyway, I shouldn't take sides."

Chloe exhaled. Unfortunately, Candi was probably right.

Gretta spoke up. "I can't officially take a stand on behalf of the Palace, obviously. But I'd put one of those signs in my yard if you've got enough."

Victory tasted so sweet. In a town like this, everyone knew everyone's house. And having Gretta publicly declare her opposition of the resort was as good as broadcasting that the Palace would not be happy about the change if it happened.

"That's perfect. I'll drop one by your house tomorrow!"

She stopped and talked to Lisa at Fresh Catch and Winona at the Eastside Cafe, and they both agreed to display the signs as well. Chloe also left Winona a plate of homemade cookies and dodged every one of the woman's questions about the exchange that had happened the other day. Throwing iced coffee at the developer everyone was talking about? Never happened.

The support from the local businesses was encouraging, and she knew that together, they could make a difference. She couldn't help but feel a glimmer of hope. Sanctuary Island was a special place, and she was determined to protect it.

Starting tonight, she'd do her best to convince him that Sanctuary was perfect as it was, but she wasn't going to sit back on her heels and assume he'd give up that easily.

As soon as the signs arrived, she would get them delivered. And surely as people saw them and started talking about the repercussions of such a large development, the SICAB meeting would be nothing but a formality.

Derrick's project would be dead in the ice-cold lake water.

twelve

DERRICK

DERRICK STEPPED INTO THE COMMUNITY CENTER, immediately feeling out of place. The fluorescent lights cast a harsh, unnatural glow over the room, and the air was thick with the smell of food, including the overwhelming scent of garlic from something he wasn't excited to find. The chatter of excited voices filled the air, punctuated by bursts of laughter and the occasional clatter of metal chairs being arranged.

He glanced around, noticing the array of long folding tables set up for the dinner. Each table was covered with mismatched tablecloths, and the chairs looked like they had been pulled from various corners of the island. Derrick's tailored jacket and polished shoes stood in stark contrast to the casual attire of the other attendees. He felt a pang of regret for agreeing to come along. This was the furthest thing from his usual scene. But if it meant Chloe would give his resort a chance, then he'd do anything.

"Derrick, over here!" Chloe's voice called out, cutting through his discomfort.

She waved at him from a table near the front. She was surrounded by people, her warm smile lighting up the room. Of course, that smile wasn't directed at him. Derrick made his way over, feeling the curious eyes of the locals on him. Chloe introduced him to a few of the attendees, who greeted him with polite, if somewhat wary, nods.

"Glad you could make it," Chloe said, her eyes sparkling with mischief. "I never miss Bingo night."

Derrick raised an eyebrow. "Looks... lively," Derrick replied, forcing a smile.

Who was this woman, and what had she done with the polished, no-nonsense chef he'd been engaged to? He couldn't help but notice the stark differences between his world and this one. The informal, close-knit atmosphere was completely foreign to him.

Chloe handed him a plate and some silverware from the bag on her chair. It was a thin white dish with a ring of blue flowers on the edge. He twirled it slowly between his palms. "What do I do with this?"

Chloe rolled her eyes. "You eat. Let's go before all the good stuff is gone."

"But the plate?"

"Everybody brings their own dishes," she explained as if that weren't the strangest thing he'd ever heard. What kind of event required you to bring your own silverware?

The front of the buffet line was adorned with a sign that read, "Fundraiser for Bella Paulsen." Next to the sign was a photo of a young girl with a bright smile and a bald head, clearly in the midst of a battle with leukemia. Beside the photo was a donation bucket—an empty gallon of ice-cream, with a large slit cut in the top.

Chloe noticed his gaze and leaned in close. "Bella's a sweet girl. Her family has been struggling to cover the travel expenses to the Mayo Clinic. That's what tonight's fundraiser is for." She dropped a few bills in the bucket. "Dinner's on me," she said, then pushed him down the line.

Derrick felt a lump in his throat. He had been so focused on his own discomfort that he hadn't considered the purpose of the event. He glanced around the room, seeing the warmth and solidarity among the community members, all rallying to support one of their own.

As Chloe led him down the buffet table, the sheer variety of dishes laid out was staggering. Derrick eyed a steaming crockpot of chili next to a platter of deviled eggs adorned with paprika. Chloe pointed out her favorites, like Sicilia Klein's famous macaroni and cheese, its golden crust promising cheesy goodness underneath. They passed a tray of bacon-wrapped dates, their smoky aroma mingling with the sweet scent of freshly baked cornbread. If Derrick were a betting man, he'd guess that Chloe brought those. Had she done it because they were his favorite? Or was it a coincidence?

"Ooh, try this," Chloe pointed.

Derrick scooped up a spoonful of a mysterious casserole, glancing at Chloe for reassurance.

"Trust me, you'll love it," she said with a smile. "Oh, and this is Mrs. Benson's apple pie." Chloe nodded toward a pie with a perfectly-latticed crust. "It's legendary around here."

As they filled their plates, Derrick couldn't help but feel a bit more connected to this tight-knit community, each dish representing a piece of the island's heart.

Back at the table, surrounded by strangers vying for Chloe's attention, he picked at his food, trying to mask his discomfort. The din of conversation around him was a constant reminder of how out of place he felt.

There was an unexpected pang of envy at the way she belonged here.

"When are you going to share that recipe for that black bean dip, Chloe?"

Chloe grinned. "Now, now, Max. I told you. I would

tell you, but then I'd have to kill you! Oh, that reminds me. Your mom said you had some extra rock salt? I'm about out, but my front walk always refreezes overnight. Didn't you need some too, Nicole?"

She was clearly in her element, seamlessly moving from one conversation to another. Derrick watched her, admiring her ability to connect with people. It was a stark contrast to his own life, where connections were often shallow and transactional. He couldn't help but feel a twinge of jealousy, mingled with admiration.

The food was surprisingly good. He was pretty sure his plate alone had an entire stick of butter on it between the various dishes, but it felt good to eat food that had been lovingly made by a regular person–not a fancy chef. Though, he was looking forward to the bacon-wrapped dates biding their time on the edge of his plate.

"How is it?" Chloe asked.

"So good," he said between bites. "I haven't tried this one yet." He dipped his fork in the mystery casserole. What did you say it was?"

"I didn't," she replied. Then she put a whole meatball in her mouth. She smiled around it, and his own grin spread in return. No one made him smile as easily as Chloe.

He took a bite of the casserole she'd recommended and immediately froze.

The etiquette lessons his aunt and uncle had forced him into took over. The grainy texture was somehow crunchy and mushy at the same time. Resisting the urge to immediately open his mouth and spit it out, he discretely deposited the bite into his napkin. "What was that, Saucy? Are you trying to kill me?" he whispered.

Chloe tried to contain her laughter, but it quickly spilled out. "You should have seen your face. Oh my word." She smacked the table.

"What's going on over there, you two?" someone asked from down the table.

Chloe explained through her guffaws of laughter, as Derrick felt his face turn bright red with embarrassment. "He tried Gail's famous tamale pie."

Groans filtered from around the table at her announcement. Apparently, he was the butt of some big joke. "Har har, very funny. Does she bring this a lot?"

"Every time, man. Every single time." The man clapped him on the shoulder. "I'm Max, by the way."

"Derrick."

"Doesn't she realize that the casserole never gets eaten?"

Max laughed. "Nah. Everybody takes a little bit and then we scrape it into the trash with the rest of our dirty plate. She's so proud of the dish. Says the recipe came from her abuela or something. But I think something got lost in translation, you know?"

Derrick shook his head. "So you all just play along with it?"

Chloe shrugged. "I'm pretty sure she knows at this point, and now she brings it to mess with us. She'll even specifically ask you if you thought the batch was extra spicy or something. But she keeps bringing it."

After dinner, the dishes were cleared away to make room for Bingo. Derrick watched as people lined up to buy their Bingo cards—each card was two dollars. Prizes, ranging from homemade quilts from the ladies quilting circle to gift certificates to local businesses were displayed on a table near the front.

Chloe pointed at the quilt. "Believe it or not, I actually helped with that quilt. If you get close, you can probably spot my awful uneven stitches."

"Quilting, Saucy? I never would have put money on that."

"The winters are long around here," she said with a shrug, color rising in her cheeks.

"I'm going to run to the restroom before we get started," he said.

Afterward, he made his way to the donation table. He discreetly pulled out his wallet and slipped whatever cash he had into the bucket. He wasn't sure how much was there, but he hoped it would make a difference. Unsatisfied with the amount, he also sent a text to Shaun instructing him to find the best way to anonymously donate to the little girl's family.

As he turned back, he caught Chloe's eye. She had seen him, and for a moment, their eyes locked. There was no need for words; the smile she tried to hide said it all.

When he got back to the table, Chloe handed him a Bingo card and a dabber. "You ready?" she asked, a playful glint in her eye.

"Ready as I'll ever be," Derrick replied, trying to match her enthusiasm.

As the Bingo game began, Derrick found himself surprisingly engaged. The room was filled with the sound of numbers being called out and the excited murmurs of players checking their cards. Chloe was fully immersed, laughing and chatting with those around her. Again, Derrick couldn't help but feel a little envious of her easy rapport with the community, and wish that she would be that carefree and vibrant when she was talking to him.

He slowly relaxed, the initial discomfort giving way to a sense of belonging. He even managed to win a round, earning a homemade pie as his prize. The cheers and applause from the others felt strangely satisfying. They celebrated his win as though he were a part of their group.

As they started the next round, his phone buzzed. Shaun's name displayed above a text message.

SP: HoH Gala?? Jess is breathing down my neck. I can't believe you promised you would bring a date. Why would you do that?

Derrick grimaced. His assistant asked a valid question. He wasn't exactly sure why he'd promised the coordinator that he would have a plus one. It had something to do with the fact that he was being honored at this year's gala, something he had fruitlessly tried to insist they not bother to do.

When he'd agreed to bring a date–almost six months ago–he'd been sure he could beg off as the event got closer. But Jess didn't become the most respected and feared fundraising coordinator in the city by letting things slide.

DW: She'll survive with an empty chair at my table.

SP: She's threatening to name next year's gala the Derrick Webster Gala of Hope if you don't bring a date.

Derrick paled. The woman was terrifying, and her negotiation skills were better than most CEO's he'd dealt with.

He glanced across the table at Chloe. Would she consider… Nope, there was no way. She hated him.

She lifted her eyes from her bingo card and gave him a questioning look. "What's wrong?"

He shook his head. "Just a work thing. Nothing I can't handle."

Chloe snorted. "Yeah, I bet."

"What's that supposed to mean?" He couldn't help but ask the question.

Chloe shrugged, her cheek pulling up in a twist. "You've always got everything handled, don't you?"

A crease formed between his eyebrows. "You say that like it is a bad thing."

"Tell me the last time you had a problem and didn't have a solution for it," she said, a challenge in her voice.

He took the bait. It seemed like he always took the bait when Chloe was involved. "Actually, I don't have a solution for the problem Shaun reminded me of."

"Okay, what is it?"

Derrick ran a hand over his hair, feeling self-conscious about admitting this. "I have to find a date for the Harvest of Hope Gala. It's tomorrow night and I've got nothing."

Chloe's eyebrows flew skyward. "You can't find a date? I find that hard to believe."

Derrick smirked. "Why, Ms. Bennett… Is that a compliment?"

"Hardly. I'm just saying, surely there are women stupid and desperate enough to date you."

He ignored the temptation to point out that she had previously dated him. Extensively. "Ah, yes. There most certainly are. But every single one of them would have me stabbing myself with my steak knife during the second course just to end the night quicker."

Her laugh filled the space between them. Knowing the kinds of women who typically chased him, he'd only been halfway joking. But Chloe's laughter filled him with a desperate desire to hear it again.

"Come with me," he blurted out.

Chloe choked on the sip of lemonade she was taking. "What?"

"Come with me to Chicago for the gala tomorrow."

She looked at him like he was insane. "Why on earth would I do that?"

Agh. He'd forgotten that piece of things. She still hated him. "I'll give you $10,000."

She glared at him. "I'm not an escort, so don't you dare try to buy my company."

Derrick hung his head, appropriately chastised. "I'm sorry. I'm just… What can I do? I really would like you to come with me."

Chloe was quiet for a long time. "Can I stay another two days after the gala? You don't have to stay, but you'll need to get me home when I'm ready."

"Deal," Derrick immediately agreed. Whatever it took, he would agree to it. "Yes. My plane will be at your disposal." He briefly wondered why she needed to stay in Chicago, but then dismissed it. She was trapped here on this isolated island all winter. She probably wanted to shop or see friends. The woman had resorted to quilting, for crying out loud. If that wasn't a cry for help, he didn't know what was.

Chloe inhaled and stayed silent for another beat. He held his breath as he waited for her decision.

"Okay, I'll go."

Derrick released a forceful breath. "Thank you. Seriously. I mean it."

"Don't make me regret this. We're only going as… frenemies or whatever."

Frenemies or whatever felt like a good way to define it.

As the evening drew to a close, Derrick looked around the room, a deep sense of respect for the community filling him. They had welcomed him, despite his initial awkwardness and brash methods. Tonight's event was what Sanctuary Island was all about: people coming together to support one another.

"Thank you for coming tonight, Derrick," Chloe said as they gathered their things. "It means a lot, not just to me, but to everyone here."

"I can see why you love it here," Derrick admitted, a newfound appreciation in his voice. "This was pretty special."

Chloe smiled, a hint of melancholy in her eyes. "The whole place is. And that's why we have to protect it."

Derrick nodded, understanding her sentiment more deeply than ever before. How could he make her believe that his plan for the resort wasn't going to ruin their way of life?

They walked out into the crisp night air, the stars twinkling above them. Derrick was still determined to move forward with his plans for the resort when they returned, but he knew he needed to approach things differently. Sanctuary Island had a spirit that needed to be respected, and he was beginning to see that the path forward required more than financial moves; it required heart.

And the three days in Chicago with Chloe? He wasn't sure what that would require, but it certainly wouldn't be boring.

thirteen

CHLOE

Chloe stepped out of the sleek black car, her eyes widening at the sight of Derrick's Chicago mansion. It was grand, almost overwhelming in its opulence. When they dated, he'd had a sleek condo in the city. When had he moved here?

The sprawling estate was surrounded by manicured gardens, and the mansion itself stood as a testament to luxury, with its towering columns and ornate facade. She'd thought the private jet had been over-the-top, but this was next level. Chloe swallowed hard, reminding herself that this was just for two nights.

She was just here because Derrick had the ability to get her to and from Chicago for the Raven Foods partnership. And if tolerating him at the Harvest of Hope Gala was what it took to take advantage of that opportunity, then that was what she was going to do. She'd brought all her camera gear, and her best dress for the gala. Though, her closet wasn't exactly built for events like this anymore.

At least Derrick had ignored her on the flight. He'd been on his computer the entire time or deep in conversation with Shaun. And he'd been dropped off at the office while the driver brought her here alone.

A butler greeted her at the door, leading her through the opulent hallways. Crystal chandeliers sparkled overhead, casting a warm glow on the marble floors. Finally, they reached a beautifully appointed guest room, where the butler opened the door with a flourish.

"Miss Chloe, everything has been prepared for your comfort," he said with a polite bow.

Chloe stepped inside, her breath catching at the sight. The room was stunning, decorated in soft creams and golds, with a large four-poster bed draped in luxurious linens. On the bed lay a gorgeous evening gown, shimmering under the soft light. Next to it, a pair of delicate heels and a box of jewelry waited to complete the ensemble.

This was too much. This was just a business deal. Her eyes trailed the designer gown, feeling slightly nauseous at the idea of wearing something that was worth as much as her house on Sanctuary Island.

Before she could fully take it in, a friendly-looking woman entered the room, carrying a tray of beauty products. "Hello, Miss Chloe. I'm Jane, and I'll be helping you get ready tonight. But first, let's start with a nice, relaxing bath."

"Oh, no. I'm fine," she protested.

"Mr. Webster insists," the woman said.

Jane guided her to the bathroom despite her protests, where a large tub was already filled with fragrant bubbles. Well, since it was already drawn, refusing it would be wasting water, right?

Sure. Whatever she wanted to tell herself. Chloe slipped into the warm water after Jane left, letting out a sigh of relief as the tension of travel melted away. The scent of lavender filled the air, calming her nerves. She leaned back, closing her eyes, and allowed herself a moment of indulgence.

After what felt like blissful eternity, she climbed out, wrapping herself in a plush robe that had been laid out for her.

She stepped out of the bathroom and found Jane waiting patiently. "Feeling better?" she asked with a smile.

"Much," Chloe admitted.

Directing her to a dressing table, Jane began to work on Chloe's hair and makeup. Chloe watched in the mirror as her hair was styled into elegant waves and her makeup was applied with a delicate touch. Jane's skilled hands transformed her, highlighting her features and making her feel more beautiful than she had in a long time. She'd still rather be in a messy bun and a splattered apron, but this was a nice change of pace.

"There," Jane said, stepping back to admire her work. "You look absolutely stunning." She looked at her watch. "I'm very sorry, but I do have to go. I have another appointment this afternoon. Mr. Webster will be waiting for you at six. You'll want to wait until then to put on the dress to avoid wrinkles."

Jane left and Chloe was left alone in the room with her thoughts. This was surreal. She knew her life had been more like this six years ago, but it felt so foreign to be here, having her hair and makeup done, with a designer gown waiting for her.

When it was finally time, she slipped it on. She reached her arms around to her lower back and tugged the zipper up as far as she could reach. Then she tried from her shoulders, but couldn't reach the elusive pull. She was breathing slightly heavy when she finally gave up.

She caught a glance of herself in the mirror. It was a stunning piece, the kind of dress that made Chloe feel like she had stepped out of a fairy tale. The fabric was soft and flowing, hugging her curves in all the right places. The dark-navy blue was striking against her skin, which was nearly colorless after a northern winter. She felt like a princess.

Chloe looked at herself in the mirror, hardly recognizing the woman staring back. She took a deep breath, trying to steady her racing heart. This was only one night, she reminded herself. Just one night of pretending.

As she made her way downstairs, she saw Derrick waiting at the bottom, his eyes lifting to meet hers. His reaction was immediate, his expression shifting from casual interest to mesmerized awe. Chloe felt her cheeks heat under his intense gaze.

She held her breath, waiting for him to say something, anything about how she looked. His eyes were dark as they drank her in.

"Are you ready to go?" he said, his voice low and husky.

A wave of disappointment crashed through her. "Oh, um, yeah," she replied, trying to keep her words even, though every muscle in her body felt taut like a bowstring. "I need a little help with the zipper."

After a moment of hesitation, Derrick stepped forward, his fingers brushing against her skin as he zipped up the last bit of her dress. Chloe shivered at the contact, her pulse quickening. His touch was gentle, as if he could barely stand to touch her. She could feel the heat of his body so close to hers.

"There you go," he murmured, his breath warm against her neck. Her knees wobbled in response.

Chloe turned to face him, finding herself lost in his eyes. No, it wasn't that he couldn't stand her. There was a chemistry between them that was impossible to ignore, a magnetic pull that drew them closer. She had to remind herself why she was here, why she couldn't let herself fall for him again.

"This is one night," she said, her voice trembling slightly. Was she reminding him, or herself?

"One night," he echoed, his gaze never leaving hers. His jaw was clenched and his face held an expression she couldn't decipher.

They stood there for a moment, the air between them charged with unspoken tension. Chloe's mind was a whirlwind of conflicting emotions. She hated that he had this effect on her, that he could make her feel so vulnerable and yet so alive at the same time. She had to stay focused, had to remember that this was nothing more than a necessary evil so she could attend the Fork to Factory influencer tour.

"I'm not forgiving you," she whispered. "And this doesn't mean I want your resort on my island."

His eyes flickered with something, but he gave a curt nod of acknowledgement. Derrick offered her his arm, and she took it, shoving her thoughts away from the solid feel of his bicep under her hand. The limo ride was filled with a charged silence, each of them lost in their own thoughts. Chloe kept stealing glances at Derrick, trying to read his expression, but he remained inscrutable. When they arrived at the event, the flash of cameras greeted them, and Derrick's hand tightened on hers. He led them down the red carpet, waving a hand to the paparazzi while ignoring their questions.

Inside, Derrick kept Chloe close, introducing her to important people, his hand resting lightly on the small of her back. Despite the crowd and the noise, she couldn't shake the feeling of being on display. She caught the surprised glances, the hint of recognition as people connected her with the woman who'd been on Derrick's arm years ago. Questions went mostly unasked, though some snarky women couldn't keep their claws retracted.

"Dare!" The whiny, nasally tone immediately grated on Chloe's nerves from the busty brunette who was suddenly clinging to Derrick's arm.

She called him Dare? Seriously?

"Did you resort to bringing your cousin? I told you to call me," she whined, her voice crackling like some modern day take on the Valley girl accent. The brunette tipped her head and ran a hand down Derrick's chest.

The white-hot spear of jealousy careening through

Chloe's chest in response was surprising. Not to mention entirely misplaced. She had no claim on Derrick–not anymore.

"Diamond, this is Chloe. She's an old friend," he explained. That had been the line all night. An old friend. She supposed that was easier to explain than ex-fiancée, former best friend, current enemy. "I'm pretty sure I told you that we wouldn't be attending events together. It sends the wrong message."

"And what message is that, Dare Bear?"

Chloe gagged a little at the nickname.

"That I have any interest at all in a romantic future with you," Derrick stated plainly, his face lacking any emotion beyond a hint of frustration he was keeping disguised. But Chloe could almost sense it. He looked across the room behind Diamond, catching someone's attention. He pressed his hand into Chloe's lower back, guiding her away from the woman currently trying to burn her to ash with a glare.

"Enjoy the gala," Chloe said with a saccharine smile, looking back as they left. Diamond's face grew red as she gaped, apparently blaming Chloe for Derrick's lack of interest.

"If you want me to go, just say the word, *Dare Bear*," she offered sweetly. "I wouldn't want to get in the way of you and Diamond."

Derrick scoffed, and his hold tightened. "Don't you dare leave my side," he grumbled.

Chloe's cheeks heated at the pleased feeling his words created in her chest.

As the evening wore on, Derrick's behavior toward her was impeccable. He was attentive, charming, and made sure she was comfortable at all times. Even if his own discomfort was nearly palpable. Chloe could almost feel how much he'd rather bail on this event. Was it because of her?

When the server delivered her dinner, he also set a small ramekin next to her plate. "Your special request, ma'am."

She gave a questioning glance to Derrick before directing her question to the server. "What's this?"

"This is an extra serving of the peppercorn sauce that is being served with the steak tonight, as requested."

Chloe raised her eyebrow. "Thank you," she said to the young man, who seemed to be getting nervous. "Explain," she demanded, her eyes never leaving Derrick's face.

A hint of a smile played on his lips. He shrugged. "I just thought you'd want extra. That is why I started calling you Saucy, after all."

Chloe pressed her lips together, trying not to let the

sweet gesture unravel all the walls she'd been desperately trying to keep intact tonight. He wasn't wrong, but it was such a particular detail for him to remember about her preferences. There was never enough sauce on fancy plates of food. She wanted her pasta swimming in it.

Or, in this case, her steak.

She dipped a bite of it into the peppercorn sauce and slid it off the fork, hiding her smile behind the action.

During the presentation after dinner, Derrick's unease became even more pronounced. He fidgeted in his seat again, distracting her from the speaker, Jess something.

"Sit still," she hissed in his ear.

"Each year, we like to take a moment to recognize some of the most significant of our donors. Now, this year, I'm extra excited about this one. I've been on staff at Harvest of Hope here for going on five years, and in that time, there isn't one single organization or person who has done as much for Harvest of Hope as the man we want to recognize tonight. Now, I've been forbidden from saying exactly how much money our honoree has donated, but I can assure you that whatever you're thinking, you need to add a few more zeroes to it." Chuckles filled the room, and Chloe's gaze slid to the man next to her, thinking of the donation he'd made to Bella's fundraiser.

"But it isn't only the financial support. As a member of our Board of Directors, he has provided incredibly valuable insight into our operations, initiatives, and strategic planning. He's also clocked an impressive number of volunteer hours for someone who claims to be too busy any time I try to set him up with my sister."

More laughter skittered through the crowd. Chloe had to admit, this lady was good. She was lauding their donor while keeping this lighthearted and entertaining.

"I'd like to welcome to the stage this year's Volunteer of the Year, Derrick Webster!"

Applause filled the room and Chloe's mouth fell open. Derrick stood and stepped away from the table. As she watched in awe, Derrick good-naturedly accepted the honor and highlighted the importance of the programs by telling a few stories of children he'd met through his time working with Harvest of Hope.

"There's one other person that I have to thank. Because without her, I never would have paid attention to Harvest of Hope. I'm actually pretty self-centered."

The crowd was eating up his self-deprecating humor, but Chloe felt like she was watching a car accident and couldn't tear her eyes away. "My friend Chloe has always been passionate about feeding people as a way to build connections with, care for, and encourage people. Good food doesn't just nourish the body, she says. It feeds the soul."

His eyes met hers from the podium, and Chloe sucked in a shaky breath. "It was her interest in Harvest of Hope's initiatives in her old neighborhood that pushed me to get involved all those years ago. So… I guess I hope she's proud of the work we've been doing all these years."

Lastly, he encouraged everyone in attendance to give even more by offering to match all of tonight's donations.

As he stepped off the stage, Chloe felt the cool tracks of the tears that had spilled over her lashes. She swiped at them, careful not to smudge the eyeliner Jane had so expertly applied.

Derrick returned and she flashed him a look that carried years' worth of questions. She had no idea that he was so involved with Harvest of Hope. And it made her feel all kinds of ways she couldn't afford to feel.

He leaned in close, his lips brushing her ear. "Are you okay? Are you having a good night?"

Chloe turned to him, her eyes searching his. "It's... different," she admitted.

"Different good or different bad?" he asked, a hint of a smile playing on his lips.

She couldn't help but smile back. "Different good, I think."

He laughed softly, the sound sending shivers down her spine. "I'm glad to hear that."

As the night drew to a close, Derrick led her outside to a quiet terrace overlooking the city. The view was stunning, the lights of Chicago sparkling like stars. Chloe leaned against the railing, trying to gather her thoughts.

"Thank you for coming tonight," Derrick said, his voice sincere. "It meant a lot to me."

"Why?" she asked, turning to face him. "Why did you want me here?"

"Other than fending off the wolves like Diamond?" he quipped.

Chloe raised an eyebrow. He didn't really need her for that. And truthfully, her presence had barely made them pause. These women were vipers.

He hesitated, his gaze locking onto hers. "One, I really did need a date that wouldn't make me miserable. But also… I wanted you to see this part of my life. I wanted you to understand."

"Understand what?" she pressed, her heart pounding.

"That I'm not the man you think I am," he said softly. "There's more to me than just business and ambition. I'm not heartless."

Chloe's breath caught at the raw honesty in his voice. For a moment, she saw a glimpse of the Derrick she had once loved, the man who had captured her heart. But then the reality of their situation came crashing back, and she had to remind herself to stay guarded.

"This doesn't change things about Sanctuary," she argued, her voice barely above a whisper.

"Give me a chance," he pleaded, his eyes searching hers. "That's all I'm asking."

She looked at him, torn between her desire to believe him and her fear of being hurt again. "We'll see," she said finally, her voice wavering.

Derrick nodded, accepting her answer. "Fair enough."

They made their way back to the car. The walls she had built around her heart were starting to crack, and she wasn't sure if she had the strength to keep them up. All she knew was that being with Derrick made her feel things she hadn't felt in a long time, and that terrified her more than anything.

Back at the mansion, as Derrick walked her to her room, the silence between them was filled with unspoken words. When they reached her door, he paused, his hand lingering on the handle.

"Good night, Chloe," he said softly, his eyes locking onto hers.

"Good night, Derrick," she replied, her heart aching with the weight of everything left unsaid.

As she closed the door behind her, she leaned against it, trying to steady her racing heart. Tonight had been a whirlwind of emotions. It was as if everything had been laid out to weaken her resolve. But she couldn't let that happen. Sanctuary Island meant too much to her to let deep pockets and designer dresses change her mind.

fourteen

CHLOE

CHLOE SET THE BASKET OF SCONES ON THE TABLE AND double-checked that the juice and coffee were set up. The morning sun filtered through the lace curtains of the dining room, casting a warm glow on the neatly set table. The aroma of freshly brewed coffee mingled with the scent of sausage and blueberry pancakes, filling the room with a welcoming fragrance.

After three days away, it was nice to be back here. The last two days at Raven Foods had been a dream. She had so much video footage to edit, it would take her months. But they were paying her for one video every week for the next three months, with an option to extend if they liked her content.

In the back of her mind, she'd been brainstorming what kinds of videos she would make combining her time in the kitchen with the footage and information she'd received at their factory. Meeting Fiona Raven had been pretty spectacular also. The petite brunette culinary icon was feisty and inspiring.

Chloe wanted to be her when she grew up.

She checked her watch, then returned to the kitchen, realizing that Derrick would be down any minute. The problem was that, instead of making her angry, a hum of excitement vibrated throughout her body at the idea of seeing him. He'd come back to Sanctuary the day after the gala, leaving her to float around his giant mansion alone.

She plated the breakfast in the kitchen, and within a few minutes heard the quiet conversation of Derrick and his assistant as they fixed their coffee and settled into their seats at the table.

She placed the finishing touches, adding a dollop of whipped cream on top of the blueberry compote that adorned the pancakes. She grabbed the plates and pushed through the door to the dining room. This time, Derrick had chosen a chair facing the kitchen. He greeted her with a smile. It was unfair the way his green eyes seemed to pierce right through her defenses, glinting with a mix of mischief.

"Good morning, Saucy," he said, his lips teasing as he used the old nickname.

His rugged jawline and the way he carried himself

with an effortless confidence only made it harder to keep her emotions in check. Every time he looked at her like that, memories of their past resurfaced. Happy, butterfly feelings that were chased by heartbroken, wounded bird feelings. She didn't know what to do with the emotions.

Just like it had the other night when she'd seen Derrick discreetly slipping a not-insignificant amount of cash into the donation bucket. She'd been surprised by the gesture, expecting him to be the indifferent, business-focused man she had painted him to be. Like the Harvest of Hope. And that was a long-term thing, too, not an easy one-time gift. His generosity confused her, and she found herself further questioning her assumptions.

It was easier when she could put him firmly in the box labeled "selfish, cold-hearted jerk."

Chloe forced a smile, trying to ignore the flutter in her stomach as their eyes met. "Good morning," she said, her voice cheerful despite the turmoil inside her. "Good morning," she said, acknowledging the other man as well. As though her entire body wasn't zeroed in on every muscle of Derrick's large frame.

Shaun lifted a hand in response.

"Smells amazing in here," Derrick said, reaching for a scone.

She carefully set the plates in front of the two men. "I hope you're hungry. We've got quite a spread today."

Derrick caught her arm with his hand as she moved to pull away. "I've never regretted eating anything you've given me."

Chloe felt a flicker of the old feelings she once had for him, but she quickly tamped it down. She couldn't afford to get emotionally involved. He let his fingers trail off her arm as she pulled away.

She gave a cheeky grin, attempting to create distance with humor. "Well, other than Gail's casserole, right?"

His laugh was relaxed and carefree, bouncing through the room. "Well, on one hand, I wouldn't choose to eat it again. On the other… it made you laugh. And it had been far too long since I saw that. It was worth it."

Chloe had hummingbirds in her stomach at that statement. Derrick couldn't say things like that to her!

"Oh," she stammered, searching for words while her mind had hit the repeat button on that sweet statement instead of being helpful and providing the essential things. Like words. Or Air.

"Enjoy your breakfast," she squeaked, beelining for the door to the kitchen.

When she was safely on the other side, she rested her elbows on the counter and hung her head.

"Hey."

Chloe yelped and straightened, banging her head on the shelf above the prep surface.

"Oh, sugar snaps, that hurt," she said, wincing and rubbing the back of her head with her palm. She turned to find Marissa watching her with a sympathetic wince.

"I'm sorry, I didn't mean to scare you."

Chloe shook her head. "I'm okay. I got lost in my thoughts."

Marissa gave her a knowing look. "Thoughts about the handsome billionaire in the dining room right now being grilled by his assistant about why he called you Saucy?"

Chloe's face heated with embarrassment. "He's not a billionaire," she mumbled.

Marissa scoffed. "You keep telling yourself that, Chloe. I don't care if he's got eight zeroes on his bank account instead of nine, it's still beyond my comprehension. I'm more curious about what has you holed up here trying to stare holes in the stainless steel."

Chloe sighed. "He's just… seeing him after all this time? It's making me remember why I fell for him in the first place. But I know where it ends, and I can't go back there."

"Oh, sweetie. I'm sorry. Here I am, teasing you about it. I'm sure it's not easy to have all these old feelings stirred up."

Chloe walked into the hug that her friend offered. “Thanks, Mare.”

What she didn’t add was the fact that, while it was hard to deal with the old feelings, it was the new feelings that had her the most worried.

She stayed polite and professional when she checked on the men mid-meal, ignoring the way Derrick watched her. After they were finished and had left the dining room, she began clearing the dirty dishes and setting from the large table.

Shaun’s voice carried through the hallway as he approached the space. “Here, let’s see if we can roll these out in here.”

He came in carrying a large rolled-up blueprint and a laptop. “Do you mind if we work in here for a bit?”

Derrick came in a few moments later, his eyes instantly finding her own.

She pulled her gaze back to the table. “Oh, sure,” Chloe replied. “Let me finish wiping this down for you.”

“Perfect, thank you so much,” Shaun said. He turned to Derrick. “So, I talked to the architect about the changes we discussed, but she had a few questions, so I wanted to run them past you.”

Derrick’s demeanor shifted instantly, the businessman mask slipping back into place. “Absolutely. I would love to have the updates done before the meeting next week. Will she be able to rush them over the weekend? It's already Friday."

Chloe's heart sank. The reminder of his project brought back the reality of their situation. She finished wiping the polished surface and stood up, forcing a smile. "I still need to put away the rest of these things." She gestured to the side table where the fresh juices were set up.

"Don't mind us at all," Derrick said with a carefree smile.

She busied herself wiping the outside of the glass carafes and pretended not to listen or watch the two men.

Shaun spread the blueprints out on the dining table, securing the corners with coffee mugs from the coffee station. "We've got the preliminary layouts here," he said, pointing to various sections. "But with the changes you wanted to make on height, we're running into a capacity issue."

Derrick leaned over the table, scrutinizing the plans. "We'll expand the rooms out this direction. We need to ensure the views are unobstructed," he said, tracing a line with his finger. "Especially from the upper floors. Obviously, even in the winter, the water view is the most desirable, but if we can have views of the forest as well, that's preferable to views of the activities area."

Chloe paused in the doorway, juice in each hand, her chest tightening. All she could envision when they spoke was the potential loss of the island's charm, the commercialization of a place that felt like home to her.

She cleared her throat, drawing their attention. "I'll be wrapping things up in the kitchen. If you need anything, just let me know."

Derrick looked up, his eyes softening. "Thanks, Chloe."

She nodded, forcing another smile before turning away. As she walked back to the kitchen, she felt a mixture of emotions—confusion, anger, and a lingering sadness. Derrick's generosity and sincerity had shown her a side of him she wasn't expecting, but his presence here, with his plans to change the island, reminded her of why she needed to keep her distance.

Chloe busied herself cleaning the rest of the kitchen, before pulling out meat for the evening reception and tomorrow's breakfast. She tried to push Derrick from her mind. But as she worked, snippets of their conversations kept creeping back into her thoughts. The way Derrick had genuinely seemed to care about Bella's plight, the way he had fit in, despite being an outsider. It was disconcerting to see him in a different light. He'd always seemed to embrace the lifestyle afforded to him as the heir to the Webster Hotel fortune. And it had been easy to get swept along in the glamour of five-star restaurants and chauffeured drivers in the busy Chicago streets. But eating a potluck with Derrick in a run-down community building with linoleum floors–and seeing the way he had opened up to the community while there... Yeah. That would be hard to forget.

It was almost as devastating as the sight of him in a tux, in his element on stage at a ten-grand-a-plate fundraiser.

After the kitchen was clean and the early prep was done, Chloe popped into the hallway directly across from the kitchen, choosing to bypass the dining room. She stopped by Marissa's desk. "I'm headed out for a few hours. I'll be back to prep the rest later."

"Sounds good. Did you see my note on the menu that we have another reservation tonight?"

Chloe nodded. She'd already set out enough bacon for the additional guests.

She headed for the back entrance, grabbing the signs she'd tucked behind the bushes next to the door this morning. With the impromptu trip to Chicago, she hadn't been able to get the signs up before they left. She took the morning and delivered her signs around town, happy with the way the red bold print grabbed the eye. We Support Small Business–NO MEGA RESORT!

She was even able to get a few more businesses that hadn't been open when she'd made the rounds earlier in the week, and was stopped by a handful of people who wanted signs for their yards. By the time she returned to the inn, there were only a couple of signs left. She tucked them safely behind the bushes again and stepped toward the door.

"What are you doing out here?" Derrick's voice startled her.

She turned to see him standing a few feet away, his hands in his pockets.

"Needed some fresh air," she said, trying to sound casual. Had he seen the signs? She wasn't ashamed of them, but there was a twinge of guilt at the fact that he didn't know she was on SICAB. And while she'd promised him that she would do everything in her power to stop him, saying it and him seeing it felt different.

He nodded, stepping closer. "Me too. Shaun's going over some numbers, and I needed a break."

They stood in silence for a moment, the tension between them palpable but different from before. Instead of resentment and suspicion about the resort, the tension she felt was centered on the unresolved emotions lingering from their past, and the way her new feelings were rapidly changing.

"Why did you have to come here, Derrick?" she asked softly. "I honestly thought I'd never see you again."

He sighed, running a hand through his hair. "I never

dreamed you'd be on Sanctuary Island, Chloe. There have been so many times over the years I considered having someone find you, just to satisfy my own curiosity. But I could never pull the trigger. And the longer I waited, the more I knew I'd probably find you happily married with some guy who didn't deserve you but at least made you a priority."

He looked away before continuing. "I think I didn't want to know if that was true. So I just tried to pretend you didn't exist." A harsh laugh escaped. "And then I show up here, and you've wormed your way into the only place that ever truly felt like home. Do you have any idea how that's been messing with my head?"

Chloe pressed her lips together, thinking of the way her own head had been in a complete tailspin since he arrived.

"This resort... The board at Webster is losing confidence in me. Apparently, I'm not as cutthroat as my father was." He huffed a cynical laugh. "The whole line of Family Adventure Resorts is my last-ditch effort to get them to take me seriously and that I'm willing to do what it takes to steer Webster Hotels through the next thirty years."

Chloe's heart sank. "Why would they doubt that? You've always done what you needed to. At least from where I was sitting, you always put work first."

He shrugged. "I put in the work, that's not the issue. But I don't really like being the bad guy."

Chloe's eyebrows lifted in surprise.

He laughed. "I know, I know. I'm sure it doesn't seem like that from your vantage point." He reached out, gently touching her arm. "I don't want to fight with you, Chloe. I never did."

She looked up at him, the familiar warmth of his touch stirring old feelings. "Neither did I," she admitted.

"I know I messed up. Six years ago, when I bailed on our vacation to—"

"For the third time," she interjected.

"For the third time," he conceded.

They stood there, the afternoon sun casting shadows around them, caught in a moment that felt both old and new. For a brief second, it was as if the years hadn't passed, as if they were still the same people who once dreamed of a future together.

But reality intruded, as it always did. Shaun's voice called from inside the inn, breaking the spell. Derrick dropped his hand, stepping back.

"I should go," he said, his voice filled with regret.

"Yeah," Chloe replied, her heart heavy. "Me too." She had to go finish the food for the evening reception. On weekend nights, she tried to make the food extra special.

Derrick turned toward the entrance and she took a moment to survey the garden and collect her thoughts.

"Chloe?"

"Hmm?"

"I heard The Lantern Room is open this weekend for their monthly off-season dinner service. It was my parents' favorite restaurant, you know..." He looked down, appearing slightly self-conscious, which wasn't an emotion she typically associated with Derrick. "I was wondering if you'd be willing to go with me? I got a table for tomorrow night."

Chloe's eyes widened in surprise. It was one thing to eat a potluck dinner with Derrick surrounded by rowdy locals. But The Lantern Room was the nicest restaurant on the island. The historic keeper's residence on the grounds of Solheim Lighthouse on the northeast corner of the island had been elegantly transformed into a quiet, romantic restaurant with limited tables.

"Oh, I um... Do you think that's a good idea? We're not–"

His eyes darkened slightly, but Derrick waved his hand, as though brushing away her concerns. "No, of course. I just thought... it might be nice to have a friend to go there with me. And I am supposed to see everything the island has to offer, right?" His expression was hopeful, but casual.

Chloe found herself agreeing to go, despite her reservations. "You know what? Sure. I'll go with you."

Derrick smiled broadly and then walked inside. A moment later, Chloe followed, her eyes dropping to where the protest signs were hiding against the house behind the shrubbery. Hopefully, she hadn't just made a huge mistake.

fifteen

DERRICK

DERRICK AND SHAUN WALKED SIDE-BY-SIDE AS THE MID-afternoon sun soared above of the quaint streets of Sanctuary Island. Derrick couldn't help but admire the old-world charm of the island's main streets. The roads were surprisingly narrow, giving way to small businesses, their bright awnings cheerful and welcoming.

Fresh Catch had an enormous painted rainbow trout statue in the front by their sign that appeared as though it was hanging from a fishing line. A bench was conveniently placed so you could stand on it and pretend you caught the fish. He bet the visiting kids loved that. The thought made him smile. Then a flash of red near the doors caught his eye.

Bold letters screamed, "We Support Small Business. NO MEGA RESORT!"

He felt a wave of frustration wash over him. "Who

put that up?" he muttered, more to himself than to Shaun. "Come on, let's grab lunch somewhere else. I have a feeling we might not be welcome here."

They turned back toward the town square after deciding to head for Eastside Cafe. As they strolled past Whimsical Pages Bookstore, Shaun suddenly stopped. "Derrick, look at this. Looks like they've been busy," he said, gesturing down the street.

The same sign was posted in the windows of nearly every shop they could see. Derrick's jaw tightened as he read the same message over and over again.

As they continued walking, Derrick's mind raced. Who could have orchestrated this so quickly? His thoughts immediately went to Chloe. She was passionate about the island and had a network of connections here. The realization that it could be her made his chest tighten. Admiration for her dedication and irritation at the obstacle she represented warred for position in his mind. It seemed like something she would do, but when? They'd been gone for days, and it really seemed like they were making progress together.

They passed a bike shop, where a particularly large sign was hung, spanning the width of the garage door. "Save Our Sanctuary," it proclaimed in bold, red letters. Derrick felt a pang of guilt. He had envisioned his resort bringing prosperity to the island, but these signs painted a picture of fear and resistance.

"Do you think this will sway SICAB?" Shaun asked, his voice low.

Derrick sighed, rubbing the back of his neck. "It might. They're community-focused. Seeing this level of opposition could definitely influence their decision."

Shaun nodded, his expression thoughtful. "We need to counter this somehow. How about a town hall meeting or something where we can address their concerns?"

"Good idea," Derrick replied, though his mind was only half on the conversation. His thoughts kept drifting back to Chloe. How had things gotten so complicated? They had once shared dreams of building a future together, and now they were on opposing sides of a battle for the island's soul. And even though he was pretty sure Chloe was behind these signs, he was still looking forward to dinner with her tonight. How was that for confused feelings?

He couldn't let her distract him from the goal of securing a place on the island for the flagship Family Adventure Resort.

Shaun was already making notes on his phone as they walked. "So, I'll find somewhere to host it and get the word out. Do you want people to submit questions ahead of time? I'm not gonna lie, boss. I'm a little afraid the town's going to turn all mob-mentality if we get them all in a room together."

"Don't be ridiculous, Shaun. These are just people worried about something messing with the way of life they love. SICAB might need to give approval, but the ones we have to convince are the people like Chloe."

How could he convince her though? He didn't even understand why she was so opposed to the resort, other than she liked winters on the island the way they were now. Was that all? Or was there more to it? Maybe he hadn't been listening closely enough to her concerns.

The sound of laughter pulled him from his thoughts. They were nearing Eastside Café, where Winona was chatting with a group of locals. Another protest sign was propped up in the window.

They continued their walk, deciding not to eat there either. They passed the hair salon where Candi-with-an-i was busy sweeping the sidewalk. There was no sign in the window, and Derrick felt a surge of hope.

Candi looked up and gave them a bright smile. "Afternoon, boys! Someone has raised quite a stir since they got to town. Quite the protest going on around here."

Derrick forced a chuckle. "It's... effective." How could he win over these people who were so fiercely protective of their community?

"Nothing personal, you know. Folks are only trying to keep things the way they are."

"Nothing personal," Derrick echoed, though it felt

deeply personal. He practically felt the fear and uncertainty in the air, and it only fueled his resolve. He had to find a way to show them that the resort could coexist with their beloved island, that it could enhance, not destroy, what they held dear.

Candi continued, "I'm trying to remain impartial, you know. With Terry being on the board and all. Good luck to you!"

Shaun broke the silence as they kept walking "We need a plan. Something to show them we're not the enemy here."

Derrick nodded, determination hardening in his chest. "We'll figure it out. We have to." He had always been driven, always focused on his goals, but this time was different. This time, the stakes were higher, the opposition stronger, and the personal connections deeper. "Come on," he said, pointing at The Bluebell across the square. "I think I lost my appetite. Let's go plan that town hall. It needs to happen yesterday."

He glanced back at the signs one last time, their messages clear and unyielding. This wasn't just about business; it was about hearts and homes, about a community fighting to preserve its way of life. And somewhere in the middle of it all was Chloe, a constant reminder of what he had lost and what he stood to lose again.

He tucked his hand into his pocket, fingering the

ring sitting there, feeling like it weighed far more than a few grams. He wasn't even sure why he'd picked it up while he was at the house the night of the Harvest of Hope Gala. It'd been sitting in his nightstand drawer for six years, mocking him with the reminder of his failure all that time.

He'd lain in his California King bed after the gala, reliving every moment of having Chloe back on his arm. Watching her walk down the steps of his house, seeing her slight blush each time she realized just how much he noticed about her, the intoxicating scent of her when he'd find yet another excuse to lean in and whisper in her ear.

All the memories had driven him to pull the box out and flip it open, revealing the flawless marquise-cut diamond he'd picked out for her, nestled in the velvet. The tiny battery built into the ring box died sometime last year, which was a pretty good indicator that he'd spent too much time looking at that ring since she'd left it behind on his kitchen counter. He knew every facet of it, every prong.

Usually, he stared at it and re-convinced himself that his anger toward her was righteous. Other times, he just contemplated what he'd done wrong, or dreamed up ridiculous scenarios that would land him in her life again.

Like his trying to build a resort on the island and

making her hate him even more than she already did. That wasn't exactly how the scenarios played out in his dreams. There was no way Chloe was going to trip over herself to fall back into a relationship with him. Been there, done there, got the T-shirt.

And despite his philanthropic efforts in the last five years, he was still the same guy he'd been back then. He still had too many things on his schedule, too many demands on his attention, and too much pressure on his shoulders to keep Webster Hotels at the top.

It was a life that didn't allow for lazy vacations, home-cooked dinners, or playing hooky to sleep in and cuddle. And all of those were things Chloe deserved. That and so much more.

He dropped the ring back into his pocket.

She might have been the one to leave, but he'd been the one to drive her away. So what was he doing? Even if she hadn't arranged the protest signs, she probably had one in her yard.

She had never hidden her opinion on his presence here or his project, but he had taken her to the gala and now to The Lantern Room, like there was nothing keeping them from slipping back into six years ago. If anyone from the board of directors at Webster found out that she was part of his opposition for this project and he was, for all intents and purposes, trying to date her? He'd be toast.

He blew out a heavy breath, tired of his mind swirling round and always circling back to the same inevitable truth. Spending time with Chloe made him the happiest he'd been in years. And there wasn't anything that was going to keep him from trying to steal more of it.

sixteen

CHLOE

CHLOE STEPPED THROUGH THE FRONT DOOR INTO THE foyer of The Hummingbird and Bluebell Inn, feeling a bit like a nervous teenager. She gripped her tiny purse tightly, finally understanding why they called it a clutch. She'd taken an especially long time getting ready, even curling her long blonde hair and letting it trail over her shoulders in soft waves.

"Oh, Chloe." Marissa's soft exhale came with a broad smile, and Chloe pulled back her shoulders as her confidence returned. "You look wonderful."

"Thanks, Mare. I still feel like maybe this was a bad idea, you know?"

Marissa flattened her lips. "You know what, I don't think it is. No matter what happens tonight or this week, I think you'll walk away in the end with the closure you have needed for all these years."

But when Derrick walked down the grand staircase, closure was the last thing on her mind. The man had always been able to wear a suit. She'd seen him in one more times than she could count over their relationship. But tonight, she noticed a lot of the changes in him she'd overlooked. The way the hair above his ears was showing hints of salt and pepper. And the way his shoulders had broadened in the last six years. He moved with the same confidence and swagger he'd always had, but somehow seemed more settled.

"Wow," he breathed as he reached the landing and crossed the foyer toward her. His eyes trailed up from her feet, and she swore she felt them over every inch of her body and the deep-red dress she wore. As he approached, his hands reached out, and she took them instinctively. "You look beautiful," he said, his eyes now completely focused on hers.

One heartbeat. Two. Maybe a hundred had passed, she couldn't be sure, because it seemed as though she were locked in place, lost in his green eyes.

Marissa's sigh of pleasure pulled Chloe from the moment and heat rose in her cheeks.

"Shall we?" He extended his elbow to her, and Chloe rested her hand in the crook of it.

They stepped outside into the rapidly cooling evening air as dusk descended on the island. Chloe looked up at

Derrick's profile. "I didn't even think about it. We should have asked someone to meet us at the parking area. I don't have a car to get us to The Lantern Room."

Derrick smiled. "It's all taken care of. Our ride should be here any minute."

Like clockwork, as though waiting for Derrick's very command—because of course the timing would be flawless for him—the soft jingle of bells reached her ears. A horse-drawn carriage appeared from Second Street and circled the town square, stopping in front of The Bluebell.

"Oh my goodness," she said through her laughter. "You didn't."

"I very much did," Derrick replied, a smile on his face, with a hint of a question in his eyes.

"I've lived here for six years, and I've never taken one of these rides," she admitted.

She watched with fascination as the driver, Taylor Everest, dismounted and walked to the carriage to open the door for them.

"Chloe," he said by way of greeting. The man was notorious on the island for his gruff demeanor. "Let's go. I've got other passengers waiting for me at the Palace, you know."

Derrick's expression darkened, but she placed her hand in his. "This is lovely," she said as they settled into the small carriage. It was much smaller than the ones she saw frequently during the summer.

Very intimate, in fact.

"That was quite rude of him, wasn't it? I paid the company quite handsomely for him to come all the way to the inn. I don't want him to ruin the experience."

Chloe laughed. "That's just Taylor. Don't let him get to you. If you're going to be a local here, you're going to have to learn to deal with the different... personalities we have around."

Derrick's expression shifted for a moment, then he nodded. "So I shouldn't get him fired?"

Chloe laughed. "I certainly hope you are joking, because that would not make you very many friends around here."

"Who said I was trying to make friends? Someone seems to have turned me into enemy number one anyway. So, I'm not sure there is much point." His expression was probing, but slightly mischievous.

She blushed. "Oh... Do you mean the signs?"

"Do I mean the signs?" he repeated. "Of course I mean the signs, Chloe." His voice was animated, but not unkind or angry. He almost seemed amused, which was impossible, but still. "Do you know how humiliating it was to walk through town square and come face-to-face with bold-faced declarations of my nefarious intentions?"

Chloe dipped her head, slightly chagrined. "To be fair… I distributed them before you confessed how much you hate to be the bad guy."

Derrick squeezed her hand. "Chloe, I know things have been complicated between us," Derrick began, his eyes earnest. "But I hope tonight we can simply enjoy each other's company, without letting all of this get in the way."

Chloe nodded, her heart aching with the complexity of her emotions. *All of this,* meaning his intention to irreparably change life on Sanctuary Island. But she couldn't ignore the temptation to set it aside for the night. "I'd like that."

She turned her focus to the carriage ride. The rhythmic clatter of hooves against the streets filled the air. The carriage, adorned with twinkling fairy lights, felt almost magical as it moved through the town and approached the unincorporated portion.

Chloe's eyes flickered to the familiar storefronts of Whimsical Pages Bookstore and Eastside Café, their protest signs still boldly displayed. She wondered if Derrick noticed them tonight, if he understood the depth of the community's resistance. But tonight was not about the resort or the future of Sanctuary Island. Tonight was... what? She couldn't quite define it.

Chloe's heart pounded in her chest, excitement and apprehension swirling inside her. She glanced at

Derrick beside her, his profile illuminated by the soft glow of the twinkle lights. His presence was both comforting and disconcerting. The closeness of the carriage left little room for distance, both physically and emotionally. She could feel the warmth of his body, the subtle scent of his cologne mingling with the crisp early-spring air.

She shivered, wishing she had thought to bring a coat, but it would have clashed with her dress. And wasn't that the most glaring red flag that what she had insisted wasn't a date was actually very much a date?

Derrick must have noticed the chill. He slipped out of his suit coat and slid it around her shoulders, then wrapped his arm around her and pulled her close. Instinctively, she leaned in, savoring the way it felt to be supported against him for a moment. How long had it been since she had simply let herself be held by someone for longer than a moment?

The carriage took a turn, bringing them past the Shore View Resort. Chloe's gaze lingered on the grand, albeit old-fashioned, building.

"Did I ever tell you about the time my friends and I snuck into the old golf course?" Derrick's voice broke the silence, his tone laced with nostalgia.

Chloe smiled despite herself. "You thought it would be a great idea to play golf at midnight."

Derrick chuckled, the sound rich and warm. "It was

a great idea, except for the part where they turned the sprinklers on us." His laughter faded, and she studied him as he watched the Shore View Palace go by. "I have such good memories here, they almost hurt sometimes." His confession was solemn.

Chloe's heart panged with sympathy for the young man who'd lost so much back then. She didn't have words to comfort him. Grief, even aged twenty years, wasn't something you could swipe away with the right words anyway. Instead, she put her hand in his and rested her head in the cradle of his shoulder. "They'd be proud of you, Derrick," she said softly.

He didn't answer, but his grip tightened.

The carriage continued its journey, the path now winding through a wooded area. The trees, their branches bare or stubbornly clinging to the pine needles that refuse to fall each winter, formed a serene canopy overhead. Another bend and the lake came into view, its surface golden under the sunset.

As they approached the northeast side of the island, the silhouette of the Solheim Lighthouse emerged from behind the trees. As they drew close, The Lantern Room, nestled in the historic keeper's residence, came into view, its windows glowing warmly.

The carriage came to a halt, and Derrick helped her down, his touch lingering just a moment longer than necessary. Chloe's heart raced as they walked toward the entrance. She could feel the weight of his gaze, the unspoken words hanging in the air between them.

Inside the restaurant, soft golden light spilled from crystal chandeliers, casting a warm glow over the rich mahogany tables adorned with crisp white linens and delicate floral centerpieces. The walls, lined with vintage maritime paintings and nautical artifacts, whispered tales of the island's storied past.

Floor-to-ceiling windows had replaced two walls, providing breathtaking views of Lake Huron, where the setting sun painted the sky in hues of orange and pink, creating a romantic backdrop that seemed almost too perfect to be real. The soft strains of a violin carried through the restaurant.

As Chloe followed the maître d' to their table, she couldn't help but notice the intimate, candlelit booths designed for privacy and quiet conversation. The air was filled with the tantalizing aromas of freshly baked bread and gourmet dishes being prepared by the island's top chef. Each plate that passed by was a work of art, meticulously crafted with vibrant, locally-sourced ingredients.

Chloe's heart raced as they were seated at a secluded corner table, offering a panoramic view of the lighthouse and the sunset-lit waters beyond. Derrick pulled out her chair with a charming smile, and the flickering candlelight cast soft shadows on his face as he took his seat across from her. It was undeniably romantic, and the reality of sharing such an intimate space with him was both thrilling and unnerving.

A waiter appeared, presenting them with elegant leather-bound menus and a selection of fine wines. As Chloe glanced at the offerings, she marveled at the exquisite choices: pan-seared scallops with truffle risotto, filet mignon with a red wine reduction, and an array of decadent desserts that promised to be the perfect ending to a memorable meal.

"What's your favorite thing on the menu?" Derrick asked.

Chloe gave a small smile as she studied the dishes. "I've actually never been here."

Derrick's eyebrows shot up. "Really? Why not? You're a chef. You love trying places like this."

Chloe ducked her head, feeling slightly embarrassed. "Well, it's surprisingly expensive to live here, and while I love my job at The Bluebell, it doesn't exactly pay like Chicago did."

Derrick shook his head. "I guess I still don't understand why you left. You loved your job at Bravissimo, didn't you?"

She shrugged. "I did, and I was learning a ton from Louis all the time. I loved the challenge." She hesitated, unsure how much she should reveal. "I… I loved you more, though." She rushed into the next sentence, not wanting to give him time to respond yet. "When it turned out you didn't feel the same way… I just had to get away from everything. The whole city reminded me of you every time I turned around. I got depressed and anxious. I was miserable. I started looking for somewhere that might make me happy again."

"And you came to Sanctuary Island."

She nodded, though he hadn't asked a question. "You'd always light up when you mentioned this place. The way you talked… It was like some magical, perfect place that existed frozen in time." She shrugged. "I guess I needed a little magic back then."

"And did you find it?" His eyes bore into hers, like his entire future hinged on the answer to the question.

"I did," she finally said. "I remembered who I was without you on my arm or a wedding binder in my bag." Her words didn't hold any sting, though she knew how they could be interpreted. "The people on the island took me in and embraced me as a local from the day the last ferry of the season left and I was still here. Marissa and Keith gave me a job and brought me to church with them."

Derrick's eyes widened a fraction of an inch. "Church?"

She smiled. "Yeah, church. I think the biggest thing that helped pull me out of the dark place I was in was the fact that I reconnected with Jesus. I'd forgotten my faith while we were together, and I won't let that happen again." She pressed her lips together after that statement, slightly afraid of what Derrick's response would be, then ashamed of her own lack of faith.

He surprised her by reaching for her hand. "I think that's wonderful, Chloe. You seem less… restless here and more confident. And whether that's because of the island or church or something else entirely, I don't know. But I'm really glad you're happy."

seventeen

DERRICK

"I'm really glad you're happy," he said, realizing exactly how true it was.

In the six years since he found her engagement ring and a note on his kitchen counter, he'd wished a lot of things for Chloe. At first, he'd hoped that she would come back and beg for forgiveness. Then, it was that she would regret the decision to leave him for the rest of her life. Eventually, he'd prayed that she would cease to be even a memory in his mind.

But now? Seeing her again, he realized that what he really hoped was that she'd found what she was looking for.

He just needed to keep reminding himself that she *had* found what she was looking for, and it wasn't him.

"Are you? Happy, I mean?" Chloe's quiet question

had him shifting his weight back in his chair, needing distance from her for some reason.

He lifted his cheek in a half smile. "Yeah, of course. Why wouldn't I be happy?"

Chloe nodded slowly but didn't say anything. Silence was the best interrogation technique. He knew that, but knowing what she was doing didn't help him fight the urge to keep talking. "I'm young, healthy, and I have more money than I know what to do with."

He glanced around, almost begging for a waiter to come interrupt this conversation. He glanced back at Chloe, and she still didn't say anything.

He sighed. "Stop it."

His eyes dropped as her lips quirked into a smile. Great, now he was staring at her mouth.

"Stop what?" she asked, amusement coloring her tone.

"You can't convince me that I'm not happy."

"I wasn't trying to," she said, frustrating him further.

"Do you ever think about what might have been?" he asked quietly, his gaze steady on hers.

Chloe's eyes widened slightly. "Sometimes. But I try not to dwell on it." The vulnerability in her voice surprised him.

"Me too," he admitted. "But being here with you, it's hard not to wonder." He reached across the table, his fingers brushing hers. "Chloe, I..." The words caught in his throat. How could he reconcile his feelings for her with his commitment to the resort?

It was impossible. Too much had changed, and yet not enough. He was still the driven businessman, pushing with every breath to make his father proud from the grave. And she was softer. Even more enchanting than he remembered, and somehow utterly rooted here on Sanctuary Island.

"I'm glad we got a chance to reconnect," he finished, pulling his hand away from hers. "I think we both needed that closure." With the declaration, Derrick closed the shutters on his emotions, pushing down the overwhelming draw to deepen their connection.

Chloe's expression shifted, her expression slightly more guarded as she intuitively matched his intentions. The dinner continued, the atmosphere both beautiful and bittersweet. Their conversation flowed easily, memories of shared laughter and uncompleted plans weaving through their words. Derrick found himself laughing, enjoying Chloe's company.

As they dined, Derrick couldn't help but steal glances at Chloe. She was still the same woman he had fallen in love with, yet so much had changed. He found himself torn between the warmth of their shared history and the cold reality of their opposing views.

After the meal and a decadent dessert, Derrick stepped out of the warmth of The Lantern Room, holding the door open for Chloe as she followed. The crisp night air nipped at his cheeks, the faint scent of the water mixing with the pine from the surrounding trees. They walked side-by-side, their breath visible in the cold, creating small clouds that dissipated into the starry sky. The relative warmth of the sunny spring day had faded into a chilly, dark night.

Derrick slipped his suit jacket over Chloe's shoulders, ignoring the way his fingers brushed her soft skin.

"Thank you for dinner," Chloe said softly, her voice carrying a hint of the melancholy that hung over their evening.

Derrick glanced at her, her cheeks flushed from the cold and the glow of the lanterns that lined the path. "It was my pleasure. I'm glad we did this."

They meandered down the sidewalk that wound through the grounds of the Solheim Lighthouse property, circling the house and the oil house, as well as the lighthouse tower itself. The light from the lighthouse swept rhythmically across the dark expanse of the lake, a comforting beacon in the night. Derrick's heart beat faster with each step, his mind racing with thoughts of the resort, the island, and most of all, Chloe.

The way her hair caught the light, the way her eyes sparkled with unspoken thoughts. The way she concentrated, her brow furrowed, as she topped a signature dish with the perfect garnish. It was all too easy to remember the girl he had fallen in love with, and in moments like this, he could see glimpses of her in the woman beside him. The conflict over the resort seemed distant, overshadowed by the memories and emotions that surged between them.

They reached a point where the path split, one fork leading back to the parking lot, the other winding toward the cliffside overlook. Derrick hesitated, knowing that every moment together made it harder to keep his feelings locked away. He nodded toward the overlook. "Want to take a detour?"

Chloe smiled, a shy, hesitant expression that made his heart ache. "Sure."

They continued down the path, the sound of the lake growing louder as they approached the cliffs. The waves crashed against the rocks below, a rhythmic, powerful force that echoed the turmoil inside Derrick. He wanted so badly to find a way to bridge the gap between them, to make her understand his vision for the resort was not just about business but about bringing something beautiful and lasting to the island.

As they reached the overlook, the view took his breath away. The moonlight reflected off the water, casting a silvery sheen across the waves. The lighthouse beam cut through the darkness, a steady, reassuring presence. Derrick turned to Chloe, her profile silhouetted against the night sky, and felt an overwhelming surge of emotion.

"This place is incredible," he said softly, his voice barely audible over the sound of the waves.

Chloe nodded, her eyes fixed on the horizon. "It is."

"What are you thinking about now?" he asked gently, almost afraid to break the spell.

She sighed, a deep, wistful sound. "I'm thinking about how complicated everything has become. About how much I care about this island, and about how much I might... still care about you."

Derrick's heart skipped a beat. He took a step closer, reaching out to take her hand. Her fingers were cold, but she didn't pull away.

She turned to look at him, her eyes filled with a mixture of hope and sorrow. "Derrick, I don't know how to reconcile my feelings for you with my duty to this island. It's tearing me apart."

He moved closer, their faces inches apart. "Maybe we can find a way to work together," he whispered, desperately hoping it was true.

The world seemed to shrink around them, the sound of the water fading into the background. Derrick leaned in, his heart pounding, and Chloe closed her eyes, their foreheads almost touching.

"I can't let you build a giant resort here," she murmured.

Her words pinched in his chest. In the end, she would have to accept what SICAB and the mayor decided, right? Right now, the last thing he wanted to talk about was the divide between them. He could feel the warmth of her breath, the electricity between them palpable.

"I can't let you go again," he admitted in response, closing the nearly imperceptible distance between their lips.

An instant later, a sharp beep broke the spell.

Chloe pulled back, and he fumbled for his phone, bemoaning its very existence at this moment. He glanced at the screen.

He sighed, running a hand through his hair. "Sorry, it's just a message from Shaun. Something about the new blueprints."

Chloe stepped back farther, the moment shattered. She wrapped her arms around herself, as if to ward off the chill. "It's okay. We should probably head back anyway."

Derrick nodded, pocketing his phone and cursing the timing. They walked back in silence, the tension between them thicker than ever as they reached the parking lot and climbed into the waiting carriage.

Once they were inside and Taylor had maneuvered the horses toward the town, Derrick turned to Chloe.

"I'm serious about finding a way to make this work. Not just the resort, but us."

She looked up at him. "I want to believe that, Derrick. I really do. And even if I could trust you with my heart, which is a huge if, by the way," she added with a pointed look, "it's not just about me anymore. It's about the island and the people here."

"I know," he said, his voice firm. "I promise you, Chloe, I'm not the enemy here. I want what's best for Sanctuary Island, too."

She sighed, settling into his side and resting her cheek against his shoulder. "But what if that isn't what is best for Webster Hotels?"

Derrick pressed his lips to the top of her head, but he couldn't answer.

eighteen

CHLOE

CHLOE SMOOTHED HER DRESS AND ADJUSTED HER lightweight scarf as she walked into Sanctuary Community Church. It was only a few blocks north of her house on the east side of the island, and she preferred the casual, come-as-you-are experience. The stained-glass windows glinted in the morning sun, casting colorful reflections onto the cushioned pews. Church had unexpectedly become a place of solace for Chloe over the last six years.

She exchanged warm greetings as she made her way to her usual seat. The body of believers here were like a second family to her, their faces familiar and comforting. Even during the chaos of the tourist season, she could count on familiar faces on Sunday mornings and Wednesday nights.

As she settled in, she glanced around the church, her

eyes widening in surprise when she saw Derrick seated a few rows ahead. She'd seen him at breakfast this morning, but he hadn't said anything about attending. Right now, he was chatting with Marissa, who had probably invited him. It was very common for her to invite the guests from the bed-and-breakfast. An undeniable flutter in her chest rose at the sight of him.

Chloe tried to focus on the music, her voice blending with those around her, but her mind kept drifting back to the previous night. The dinner, the walk, the *almost* kiss. It all played over and over in her mind like a song stuck on repeat. She couldn't shake the memory of how close they had come to rekindling what they once had. She prayed for the Lord to clear her thoughts and help her focus on Him.

After worship ended, the speaker's voice filled the small church. One of the elders was giving the sermon today as the lead pastor spent time with his ailing father on the mainland.

Paul Solheim spoke about God's timing, how it is always perfect and never late. As he walked through the passage, Chloe's mind was a highlight reel of the twists and turns that had brought her to this point. Her rough upbringing in South Chicago, culinary school, Derrick, their past together, and the pain of their breakup. Then their date, the way he had looked at her, and the emotions that had surged between them. She thought about the almost kiss and the aching longing it had left in her heart.

What had so clearly felt like a closed door six years ago–the end of her relationship with Derrick—had turned into an open door leading to something so much better—her relationship with Jesus. As hurt as she had been and as painful as it was to have a love that ended, it had opened her heart to a love that never would.

She couldn't deny that there was still something between her and Derrick, though. If she was honest with herself, it had never fully faded. But she also couldn't ignore the reality of their situation. Derrick was here to build a resort, a project she believed would harm the island she loved so dearly. She felt torn between her lingering feelings for him and her loyalty to the community.

Chloe's thoughts drifted to their time together, the good and the bad. She remembered the way they had laughed, the adventures they had shared, and the plans they had made for a future that never came to be. But she also remembered the arguments, the disappointment, and the heartache of their breakup. It was all so tangled and complicated.

As Paul spoke about trusting in God's timing, Chloe wondered if perhaps there was a reason Derrick had come back into her life now. Maybe there was a purpose behind their reunion, something she couldn't yet see. But as much as she wanted to believe that, she couldn't ignore the reality of the SICAB meeting looming on the horizon and the decision she would have to make.

After the service, Chloe lingered for a moment, gathering her thoughts. She saw Derrick approach, his presence like a magnetic force she couldn't resist. He smiled at her, and for a moment, all the tension and uncertainty melted away.

"Hey," he said softly, his emerald eyes searching hers.

"I didn't expect to see you here," she admitted.

His smile assured her that he wasn't offended. "Me either, actually. I haven't exactly been on good terms with the Lord. Not since the last time I was here, actually."

Chloe's eyes widened. "I didn't… I guess I didn't know that you were a believer."

He shrugged. "I was so angry and lost after my parents died. They were the ones who brought me to church. The ones who acted like He was in total control. Then He took them from me…" His voice broke off. "I turned my back on everything they taught me."

Chloe stepped closer to him, resting her hand on his

arm. "I'm sorry, Derrick. I wish… I wish I'd known. Thanks for telling me now."

Derrick's voice was gentle when he continued. "I've been thinking a lot about what the speaker said. About timing."

Chloe nodded, her heart aching with the unspoken words between them. "Me too."

He ran a hand through his hair with a sigh. "Maybe… maybe it was all for the best, you know? I wouldn't have been good for you back then, Chloe. The more I see you here, the more I realize it. You deserved better. You still do."

Her heart felt like it was being ripped apart at his words. She knew they were true, because otherwise they would have stayed together. Words escaped her and she just whispered his name instead.

He gave a tight smile, then glanced around the rapidly emptying worship center. "Do you have plans this afternoon? I've got some work to do for the town hall meeting, but I thought maybe a picnic would be nice?" He met her eyes, his expression soft and vulnerable. "I'd like to keep talking, and it's supposed to be beautiful outside."

Chloe's heart skittered at his confession. The truth was that she'd like to keep talking to him as well. It was obvious there were tendrils of his childhood faith still anchoring him, however fragile they might be, and she wanted desperately to explore them.

"I'd like that."

The smile he flashed seemed to make the entire church brighter and warmer.

As they walked out of the church together, Chloe felt a sense of bittersweet longing. She knew that the days ahead would be challenging, that the SICAB meeting would force them to confront their differences head-on. But she also felt a glimmer of hope, a fragile spark that maybe they could find a way to navigate this storm together, or at least both walk away with more peace.

She knew that she would have to make a stand, to fight for what she believed was best for the island. And as much as she cared for Derrick, she couldn't let her feelings cloud her judgment. She could care for him, maybe support his fledgling faith as a friend, even without jeopardizing her heart or her home.

For today, though, she was going to enjoy the company of an old friend and the warmth of early spring sunshine. Tomorrow would come soon enough, with enough worries of its own.

nineteen

DERRICK

DERRICK STOOD IN THE CENTER OF THE TOWN SQUARE, adjusting the blanket he'd spread out on the floor of the gazebo. The unseasonably warm March sun bathed the square in a golden light, casting soft shadows from the surrounding trees. The air was fresh, carrying the earthy scent of thawing ground. He'd managed to gather a simple picnic, complete with sandwiches, fruit, and a couple of cold sodas from the Island Market. It felt spontaneous and low-key, which was the opposite of his usual plans. But surprisingly, he didn't mind a bit.

He glanced up as Chloe approached, her smile as radiant as the day itself. She'd changed out of her church clothes into something more casual—a light sweater and jeans, her hair pulled back in a loose ponytail. Derrick's heart surged like a puppy jumping forward, eager to slip its lead; she was as beautiful as ever. Evening gowns or sweatpants didn't matter. She was utterly captivating.

"Hey," she greeted, her eyes shining with amusement. "What's all this?"

"I believe it's called a picnic," Derrick replied, motioning for her to join him on the blanket. "New concept for me, but I think I got the basics down. Google is pretty helpful."

Chloe laughed and the sound filled him with joy. "I'm impressed, Mr. Webster. I didn't know you could pull off small-town swoony so well."

He wasn't exactly sure what that meant, but it sounded like a compliment.

They settled onto the blanket, the cool floor of the gazebo seeping through the fabric. Derrick handed her a sandwich, their fingers brushing briefly. The simple touch sent a shiver down his spine. He had to pull himself together before he promised Chloe the moon. Or to cancel the plans for the resort.

"Mind if I pray?" he asked, after an internal struggle about whether or not to ask. He wanted to, but it felt awkward and unfamiliar.

Chloe's wide grin relieved all those anxieties though. "I'd love that," she said. She bowed her head and Derrick followed.

He kept it simple, thanking the Lord for the food

and the weather and the fact that their lives had intersected once again.

As they ate, Derrick found himself lost in the way Chloe's face lit up when she laughed, or how her eyes sparkled when she talked about the little joys of island life, or how she'd gotten roped into quilting club this winter.

"Do you think God really has a plan for all of us?" he asked. He hadn't been able to shake the words from the speaker at church.

Chloe shifted, her expression contemplative as she looked out toward the grassy square beyond the gazebo. "Yeah, I really do. I think… I was so determined to build my own plan, achieve my own goals, and rely on my own desires, it took coming here to realize that His plans were so much better. It wasn't until I handed over that need to perform or the selfish desires I had that I really found joy and contentment."

A low hum rolled in his throat as he considered her words. It sounded simple, but at the same time…impossible. His ambitions were everything. Who was he if he wasn't Derrick Webster, hard-working CEO? Not that it had ever brought him the kind of contentment he saw in Chloe. There was always another deal, another merger, or another quarter with another revenue target to hit.

Derrick cleared his throat, needing to shift the

conversation before the questions inside him became too much. "I wanted to ask for your help with something."

Chloe raised an eyebrow, curious. "What do you need?"

"The town hall meeting tomorrow night," Derrick began, choosing his words carefully. "I know you're not thrilled about the resort, but I'd like your help spreading the word."

Chloe's eyes narrowed slightly, skepticism creeping in. "And why should I help you with that?"

Derrick took a deep breath. "Because I want to hear your concerns, and those of the rest of the town. Your signs caught me off-guard. I have to admit, I expected to be welcomed with open arms." Chloe snorted as he continued. "Obviously, there is more to consider. So, before we talk to SICAB, I want to make sure we know exactly what the townspeople want. All of you. I'm willing to listen and make adjustments. This isn't just about the resort; it's about the community. I know how much this place means to you, and I don't want to ruin that."

She studied him for a long moment, her expression unreadable. "I can spread the word. And you can expect me to be first in line to ask my questions."

"I would expect nothing less, Saucy," he said with a smile. She'd never cowed to him before, and he'd forgotten how much he needed that. Too many people in his life just went along with his ideas without pushing back.

“I know change can be scary,” he added, his tone gentle. “But I believe this resort can bring positive change. It can provide opportunities and improve the quality of life here without destroying what makes this place special.”

Chloe didn’t respond. He desperately wanted to know what she was thinking. “Start now. Give me one of your concerns. I promise you can ambush me with the rest tomorrow night.”

A hint of a smile played on her lips. “It’s not an ambush if you know it is coming,” she mused.

Derrick tipped his head to the side. “True. I suppose the signs felt like more of an ambush.”

Chloe winced. “I’m sorry I didn’t tell you about them. I was so angry… about everything.”

Derrick knew she wasn’t entirely talking about the resort. “I’m sorry I hurt you, Chloe. I never should have taken you for granted the way I did.”

That was perhaps the hardest part about running into her again. It had forced him to come face-to-face with the wonderful woman that she’d always been. And the way his selfish behavior had hurt her.

They were close on the blanket, their fingers almost touching as they both leaned back on their palms. The remains of their picnic were still spread around them, but the only thing he could focus on was how the soft afternoon light danced in Chloe's eyes. The warmth on their skin, combined with the faint chirping of birds, created a serene and intimate atmosphere.

"I forgive you," she breathed. "I didn't think I could... but I do. And I'm sorry for the way I left. It was the only way I could."

The gentle breeze rustled the leaves of the nearby trees, sending a cascade of light and shadow's across the nearby ground. Derrick's heart pounded as he watched a loose strand of Chloe's hair catch the wind and flutter against her cheek. Without thinking, he reached out and tucked it behind her ear. Her skin felt warm and smooth beneath his fingertips, and the simple touch sent a shiver down his spine.

Chloe turned her head slightly, her eyes locking onto his. The world seemed to fade away, leaving the two of them in a bubble of unspoken words. Derrick's gaze traveled from her eyes to her lips, and he swallowed hard, feeling the overwhelming urge to close the gap between them.

He could hear the distant laughter of children playing in the park and the occasional bark of a dog, but all those sounds seemed to be coming from another world, a world outside the spellbinding circle they had created.

Derrick leaned in slightly, his breath catching as he noticed Chloe doing the same. The proximity heightened his senses; he could feel the heat radiating from her body, see the delicate rise and fall of her chest as she breathed, and hear the soft, almost imperceptible sigh that escaped her lips.

"Chloe," he whispered, his voice a whisper above the sound of rustling leaves.

"Yes?" she replied, her voice just as soft, her eyes never leaving his.

Their faces were inches apart now, the anticipation hanging thick in the air. Derrick could see the tiny flecks of gold in her hazel eyes. He felt her breath on his skin, warm and inviting, and he knew that if he moved just a fraction closer, their lips would meet.

He shouldn't do this. He should fight the temptation to drag her back into something as complicated as it would always be between them. He should walk away and recreate the distance that was between them when he arrived at the island. The look she gave then was filled with disdain and loathing. But now, there was affection and interest. Attraction.

Time seemed to stand still as they hovered on the brink of a kiss. Derrick's heart raced, excitement and fear coursing through him. He could almost taste the sweetness of her lips, could almost feel the tenderness of the moment they were about to share. It felt like the culmination of everything they had been through, a moment that could either heal old wounds or reopen them.

Her eyes flickered shut and she dragged in a shaky breath as she pulled back, shattering the moment. "I... I should go," she stuttered. "We can't.. There's something–"

"It's okay. I understand," he interrupted gently. He leaned back with a sigh, resting his head on his hands, elbows out to the side. A moment later, Chloe did the same. He stared up at the ceiling of the gazebo, where the roof decking and sturdy support beams radiated from the center pitch of the roof like the spokes of a wheel. The craftsmanship was impeccable, each beam perfectly aligned. The neat order was a direct contrast to his chaotic thoughts.

They sat in silence for a few moments, the tension slowly ebbing away, replaced by a comfortable stillness. Chloe had to go finish the evening appetizers, so they finally sat up and packed up.

They walked back to the bed-and-breakfast, side-by-side but not quite touching. He glanced at Chloe, her face illuminated by the sunlight, and felt a surge of affection. He wasn't sure where things would lead, but with every encounter, he was more confident that he didn't want to leave the island without trying to make things work with her.

As they approached the inn, Derrick turned to Chloe, his heart full, despite the awkward end to their conversation. "Thank you for today. It meant a lot to me."

Chloe smiled, a soft blush coloring her cheeks. "It was nice. I had a good time too."

"See you tomorrow at the town hall meeting?" he asked, hope lacing his voice.

"See you tomorrow," she replied, her eyes lingering on his for a moment before she turned and headed inside, clouded with an expression he couldn't identify.

twenty

CHLOE

HE WAS THE BAD GUY, SHE REMINDED HERSELF.

He broke her heart.

He's trying to ruin the island.

So maybe he seemed… different than the Derrick she remembered. They'd never had a conversation about Jesus before yesterday. And the fact that he'd prayed over their picnic was both unsettling and unbelievably attractive. Like, fan-herself-with-her-hand-when-she-remembered-it attractive.

If she could just keep him relegated to enemy number one, it would make things so much simpler. Then her heart could adamantly hold up an Absolutely-Not vote at the SICAB meeting tomorrow without feeling this uncomfortable mix of anger and hope. She could happily wave goodbye to his private plane when he left town and have no regrets.

Instead, she was feeling more and more torn.

Her fingers absently traced the handle of a coffee mug as she stared at the wall of the kitchen at The Bluebell. The day had passed in a blur of tasks, but her mind had been elsewhere—lost in thoughts of Derrick and the picnic they had shared the day before.

She replayed the moments in her mind: their fingers almost touching, the laughter, the way his eyes had softened when he looked at her. It had felt so natural, so right, as if they had slipped back into the comfort of their old relationship. Yet, underlying that warmth was a growing guilt. Derrick still didn't know she was a member of the mayor's advisory board.

Tomorrow morning, he would be facing her judgment without even knowing it.

She'd done as he asked and spread the word about the town hall meeting tonight, and it sounded like it would be quite the turnout. She knew the community's concerns, and she shared many of them. But seeing Derrick so earnest, so invested in making this work, had stirred something in her. Now that she knew the why behind his work, it was harder to see him as the bad guy. And though he hadn't admitted it, she knew that part of this pursuit was tied back to his parents and the memories he had of them here.

With a sigh, Chloe shook off her thoughts and dumped her cold coffee in the sink. The evening appetizers had been served a while ago, and it was time to head to the meeting. Grabbing her coat, she stepped out into the crisp evening air, her breath forming small clouds as she hurried down the familiar streets of Sanctuary Island.

The community center was already buzzing with activity when she arrived. Neighbors greeted each other with nods and murmured conversations, their faces set with determination. Chloe's heart sank. She had hoped for a more welcoming atmosphere, but it was clear that the community was ready to challenge Derrick's proposal for the Family Adventure Resort.

Derrick and Shaun were already there, setting up a presentation. Cupcakes from Cathy's were at a table along the back wall. People might be tentative about Webster's intentions, but no one was turning down free cupcakes.

Derrick caught her eye and smiled, a gesture that made her heart ache with the knowledge of what was to come. Chairs were set up in misaligned rows, with a podium up front. It felt like two opposing sides going to battle. It couldn't feel more different than when they'd been here for Bingo night. Then, it almost felt like Derrick could be a part of this community. But now, with him on the makeshift stage, armored in his well-pressed dress shirt and polished shoes, it felt like the gap between them was unconquerable.

By the time the meeting started, the room was packed. Chloe took a seat near the front, her stomach a knot of anxiety.

Derrick stood up, his demeanor confident but not arrogant as he approached the podium. He held up his arms, effortlessly quieting the din of conversation. "Thank you all for coming. I'm Derrick Webster, the CEO of Webster Hotels. I'm excited that you're all so invested in the future of Sanctuary Island, because I am too."

Chloe could see the effort he was putting into this, and it made her chest tighten with a mix of pride and sorrow.

"Tonight, I want to present the vision for the Family Adventure Resort, so you can hear it directly. Our goal is to create a place that offers families a unique and enjoyable vacation experience. Unlike other resorts on Sanctuary Island, Webster Hotels wants to focus on resort experiences that will draw families to the island year-round."

He launched into his presentation, outlining the resort's features, the potential job opportunities, and the projected boost to tourism. Chloe watched the faces in the crowd, seeing skepticism and curiosity in equal measure. The image of the massive resort made her stomach clench. It dominated the landscape with its sharp lines and towering structure.

When the floor opened for questions, the first few were straightforward—questions about environmental impact, traffic, and employment. Derrick handled them smoothly, his answers well-prepared and thoughtful.

Then, a hand shot up in the back. It was Cathy Schuller from Cathy's Cupcakes, a pillar of the community and a fierce protector of local businesses.

"Mr. Webster, what kind of amenities will be inside the resort?" she asked with a challenge in her words. "Will guests have access to restaurants, shops, that sort of thing?"

Derrick hesitated, a brief flicker of uncertainty crossing his face. "Yes, like all Webster Hotels, the resort will have its own dining facilities, as well as a shop with sundry items, clothing, and equipment in addition to the entertainment options. We want to provide guests with a full range of services to ensure their comfort and convenience."

A murmur of disapproval rippled through the crowd. Chloe felt a pang of disappointment. She knew what this meant for the local businesses that relied on tourism.

Another hand went up—this time, it was Elijah from the mechanic garage. "So, you're saying that people won't need to leave the resort? They'll have everything they need right there?"

Derrick nodded slowly. "Well, we want to cater to

all the needs of our guests, but there would be easy access to town so they can enjoy the local shops and restaurants as well."

"Could a family come to enjoy the resort without ever seeing other parts of the island?"

Derrick's expression tightened, so slightly that Chloe might not have noticed if she hadn't spent too many hours studying his face in the last week. "Well, technically, yes. But–"

Murmurs rose through the room as Derrick tried to speak. Chloe's heart sank further as she saw the reaction from the townspeople. They were clearly upset by the notion that the resort would isolate visitors from the rest of the community.

"What about transportation? Without a ferry, how will people even get here?"

"We're still considering all the options for transportation, but flights are always a possibility," Derrick responded. Another question came shortly after.

When the meeting finally concluded, the atmosphere was tense. Derrick's face was a mask of professionalism, but Chloe could see the disappointment in his eyes. As the crowd began to disperse, she made her way over to him.

"Derrick, I..." She struggled to find the right words.

He gave her a small, weary smile. "It's okay, Chloe. I knew this wouldn't be easy."

Her heart ached for him. Despite their opposing views, she couldn't help but feel a deep connection to the man she had once loved.

As she watched him leave the town hall, Chloe felt a wave of sadness wash over her. She had come to the meeting prepared to stand against him, but seeing him struggle had stirred something inside her. She should be celebrating the obvious blow to Derrick's efforts, dancing with joy at the clear opposition from the rest of the town. But instead, she wanted to run her fingers through Derrick's hair and reassure him that he wasn't going to fail.

She wasn't sure where this left them or what her next move would be, but one thing was clear: her feelings for Derrick were far from resolved. And tomorrow, the SICAB meeting would deepen the divide between them even further.

twenty-one
DERRICK

Derrick woke the next morning feeling the weight of disappointment from the previous night. The town hall meeting had not gone as planned. He'd anticipated resistance, but the sheer force of the community's concerns had been overwhelming. The image of skeptical faces and the murmurs of discontent replayed in his mind as he stared at the ceiling, trying to muster the energy to get out of bed.

He finally forced himself up, showered, and dressed in a crisp shirt and blazer. Today was the SICAB meeting, and he needed to be at his best. This was truly the moment he had been preparing for, the one that could make or break his entire project. It had been good to hear the town's concerns, because now he could try to address them in the SICAB meeting.

He met Shaun for breakfast.

"You ready for today?" he asked his assistant.

"I'm all good, boss. Ready to go home, for sure," came Shaun's easy reply. "How about you?"

Shaun's expression was all-too-knowing as he asked the question, his eyes shifting to the kitchen door as Chloe came through. She was quiet as she delivered their food. "Enjoy, gentlemen."

Derrick sighed. Why did this have to be so complicated? "Yeah, I'm ready to go home. Let's walk through the details one last time." They'd stayed up late after the town hall, adjusting the proposal to compensate for a few of the concerns mentioned by the townspeople. He didn't know if it would be enough.

Breakfast was delicious, as usual. He couldn't help but wonder if Chloe had made his favorite omelet as a gesture of solidarity, or if he was looking for a connection where there wasn't one. Even the small acai bowl that went with it was one of his preferred breakfast options. He briefly wondered if he could get her to plan the menu for his resort.

If it was even opened, that was. Derrick wasn't usually one to have doubts about his business dealings, but he was feeling less and less confident in his ability to close the deal here.

The meeting was slated to begin at ten, but Derrick knew he would want to arrive early. They finished breakfast, and he quickly grabbed his briefcase, double-checking that he had all the necessary documents, and headed out.

The morning air was cool and crisp and had him missing the unseasonably warm day they'd had for the picnic. The normally quiet town of Sanctuary Island was bustling with activity as he made his way to the community center. He noticed the same protest signs from the previous day still adorning shop windows and lawns, a constant reminder of the uphill battle he was facing.

As he approached town hall, Derrick's heart sank. A small crowd of twenty or so protestors had gathered outside, holding signs and chanting slogans against the resort. His shoulders tensed, but he straightened his spine, trying to project confidence and determination. He scanned the crowd, hoping to catch a glimpse of Chloe. Despite everything, seeing her always brought him a sense of comfort.

He finally spotted her near the back, talking to a few townspeople but not holding a sign herself. Relief washed over him—at least she wasn't openly protesting against him. He'd desperately wanted to kiss her at the gazebo, but she'd pulled away. Not that he didn't understand. If anything, the town hall meeting last night had shown him just how big the gap between them was. He wasn't giving up though. SICAB seemed to be full of reasonable people, and he would do everything he could to convince them.

Taking a deep breath, Derrick walked through the crowd, nodding politely to those he recognized from the town hall meeting. The protestors eyed him warily but made no move to block his path. He needed to talk with Chloe and make sure that she knew how he felt. He wanted to see what a future with her looked like, with or without this resort. He made his way toward Chloe, but the mayor stepped in front of him.

"Mr. Webster, good morning."

Derrick pulled his thoughts away from Chloe and clasped the mayor's hand with his own. "Good to see you, Mr. Mayor." He glanced around at the small group of protestors. "Didn't expect this kind of turnout," he said with a half-smile.

The mayor gave a sheepish smile in return. "I think I warned you about having to convince the community."

"It's truly been a pleasure getting to know this community better. The town hall especially was–"

The mayor's phone rang, interrupting them. He answered while giving Derrick an apologetic look. "This is Jimmy," he said. His eyes widened as the caller spoke. "I'm on my way, give me ten minutes." The mayor hung up the phone and looked back up at him.

Derrick raised his eyebrows. "Is everything okay?"

"I'm really sorry, Mr. Webster, but we're going to

need to postpone the SICAB meeting. There's been an emergency."

"No problem at all," Derrick said smoothly. "Is there anything I can do?"

The mayor looked distracted and as frazzled as Derrick had ever seen him. "No, it's...Apparently, there's a fire at the airport. I...I need to go." He looked over the crowd, indecision warring on his face.

Derrick nodded. "You go ahead. I'll let the board know."

The mayor hurried through the crowd and Derrick glanced around, looking for the best way to let everyone know the meeting needed to be postponed. A moment later, a hand was on his arm, and he glanced down to find Chloe at his side.

"Was that Jimmy you were talking to?" she asked.

He nodded. "The mayor? Yeah. Actually, could you help me? He said there is a fire at the airport and that we'll need to postpone the meeting. I told him I would spread the word. Do you know who I should talk to?"

Chloe stuck her fingers in her mouth and gave a sharp whistle. Derrick winced at the volume, then looked on with awe as Chloe commanded the crowd.

"Listen up! There's been a fire at the airport. The SICAB meeting has been postponed, as the fire chief and mayor are dealing with the aftermath. Thank you all for coming, and we'll keep you posted with the new meeting date."

The crowd instantly began talking as they turned away, the handmade protest signs lowered.

"That was… I didn't realize you could whistle like that," he said, letting his amazement show in his voice.

Chloe's laugh was melodic, and he was enchanted by her broad smile. "One of my many hidden talents, Mr. Webster."

He shook his head. "And here I thought I knew everything about you." He reached for her hand, needing to touch her.

"You wish," she teased.

The thing was, he really did. He was beginning to see that the woman he'd known in Chicago all those years ago had been the tip of the Chloe iceberg. She was so much more than he'd appreciated back then. Had she kept herself hidden or had he been too preoccupied to notice? Perhaps a little of both.

She squeezed his hand lightly before pulling away. "I'm sorry about the protestors. The town is just… scared of change."

"I understand," he replied, though the sting of their rejection still hurt. "I wish they could see the potential benefits. I'm switching my focus to the members of SICAB though. Maybe this delayed meeting is a blessing in disguise."

Chloe's expression faltered. "Maybe," she said. "Well, I better get back to the inn. We've got some new guests coming tonight." She frowned. "Well, if they can get into the airport, I guess. I should call Zach and make sure he's alright."

Derrick opened his mouth to clarify that he wasn't thankful for the fire.

Wait, who was Zach? A twinge of jealousy struck him.

Shaun appeared next to him and Chloe was already walking away.

"What's going on, boss? I was inside setting up, but someone said the meeting is canceled?"

"Postponed, not canceled," he said absently as he watched her. Derrick tore his eyes away from Chloe's retreating form. "Better call Lola and let her know we're sticking around for a little while longer."

Shaun pressed his lips together in obvious displeasure. "Yes, sir."

"We're also changing our focus. The town hall meeting was a good start, but we need one-on-one meetings with the SICAB members."

"I'm on it," Shaun confirmed.

"Mr. Webster," a voice came from behind him.

Derrick turned, recognizing Paul Solheim from his sermon on Sunday. The memory of the eloquent sermon still lingered, churning in the back of his mind since that morning. Paul jogged up the town hall steps to meet Derrick where he stood near the top.

"Mr. Solheim, right?" Derrick said, extending his hand, hanging onto the smooth, polished metal of the stair railing under his other.

"Call me Paul, please," Paul replied, his grip firm and warm as they shook hands.

"Nice to officially meet you, Paul. I really enjoyed your sermon on Sunday," Derrick said, noticing the way Paul's eyes seemed to brighten at the compliment.

"Oh, I didn't realize you were there," Paul admitted, his tone a mix of surprise and delight.

Derrick nodded. "Marissa invited me, but I was very glad I accepted the invitation. You gave me a lot to think about."

"The Lord has a way of doing that, doesn't he?" Paul replied, his voice resonating with a quiet conviction that Derrick found reassuring.

What would it be like to have the kind of confidence this man did? Paul had gray hair and eyes lined with shallow wrinkles. Derrick knew from his research that Mr. Solheim had retired from the construction industry, but the man still seemed fit enough to throw a ladder over his shoulder and climb on a roof.

Derrick smiled, feeling a sense of camaraderie. "Yes, He certainly does. Actually, since the meeting was postponed, would you be available to grab a cup of coffee and talk a bit more?" He found himself wanting to spend more time with the man, and not simply because he was a member of SICAB.

"Well, I never turn down a cup of coffee," Paul said with a smile that seemed to radiate warmth.

Derrick turned to Shaun, who was tapping away on his tablet nearby. "I'll meet you back at the inn. Can you draft an email to the board with an update on the project and our change in travel plans?"

Shaun nodded in response, barely looking up. Derrick turned back to Paul, looking forward to a relaxed conversation over coffee.

"So, where's the best cup of coffee around this town?" Derrick asked, eager to explore more of the town's charm. Despite his belief about Sanctuary needing an influx of cash during the off-season, he couldn't deny the appeal of the slow pace and unique shops.

"Not too many options, but Eastside will be open. Great coffee. Shall we?"

As they began to walk, Derrick felt a growing sense of anticipation, not just for the coffee, but for the conversation that awaited.

twenty-two

CHLOE

The aroma of freshly baked cookies mingled with the rich scent of brewing coffee as Chloe stood in her cozy kitchen. Her tiny cottage was a haven of warmth and familiarity, with sunlight streaming through the lace curtains, casting intricate patterns on the wooden floor. The soft hum of the refrigerator was the only sound accompanying her thoughts as she set the table, carefully arranging mismatched china cups and saucers, each with a story of its own.

She'd been collecting the odds and ends from estate sales all over upstate Michigan for the last several years, her favorite way to turn a trip off the island into a bit of an adventure. If she never saw a plain white square plate again after her time at Bravissimo in Chicago, it would be okay with her.

Her friends would be here soon, for one of their

sporadic book club meetings. It had been too long since they all had a proper catch-up. When they had dinner at Fresh Catch a few weeks ago, she hadn't even known that Derrick was the visiting real estate investor.

Her mind flicked through all that had happened since then. The confrontations with him had somehow turned into a laugh-out-loud Bingo night and then to Chicago and intimate dinners and a romantic picnic. She knew she had to tell him that she was a member of SICAB, but it never seemed like the right time.

If he knew that she was one of the members of the town who had the power to approve or veto his project, she wasn't sure what he'd do. Would he try to leverage their still-fragile relationship? Would he distance himself?

The doorbell rang, startling her out of her reverie. She wiped her hands on her apron and hurried to the door, opening it to the familiar, smiling faces of Angelica, Lisa, and Jo. Behind Jo, her daughter Samantha held a small craft case.

"Hey, Chloe!" Lisa greeted her first, pulling her into a warm hug. Her perfume, a subtle blend of jasmine and citrus, was comforting and familiar.

"Hi, guys! Come in, come in," Chloe said, stepping aside to let them in. Angelica entered next, her aviator sunglasses perched on top of her head and a confident stride that spoke volumes about her personality.

"It smells amazing in here," Angelica said, her voice as vibrant as her personality.

Jo was the last to enter, with Samantha behind her. Jo's quiet demeanor was a stark contrast to Angelica's. She gave Chloe a shy smile, her eyes twinkling with warmth. "I hope it's okay I brought Sam. Gail had something come up last minute."

The front door opened directly to the living room where a fire crackled in the hearth, adding to the cozy atmosphere. "No problem at all. Hey, Sam. Come on in. I've got some cookies in the kitchen, but I haven't tasted them yet. Think you can be my taste tester?"

Sam smiled broadly, dashing through the house toward the kitchen.

The women settled into the comfortable chairs, their voices blending into a chorus of laughter and conversation. Sam settled in with her tablet at the kitchen table, perfectly content to ignore the adults in the room as she opened her craft kit to make a friendship bracelet.

"Coffee or tea?" Chloe asked, heading back to the kitchen.

"Coffee for me, thanks," Angelica called after her. "I had a flight at five this morning." She groaned.

"Tea, please," Lisa said, while Jo opted for coffee as well.

Chloe returned with the tray, balancing the

steaming mugs and a plate of cookies. "Here we go," she said, setting it down on the low coffee table. "Help yourselves."

"Goodness, it feels like ages since we had book club. I don't even remember what book we were supposed to read," Chloe joked.

"Oh, I thought we gave up on the book part of book club a long time ago," Lisa laughed. "Maybe we need to change the name."

"I think you're right," Jo said. "Who has time to read, anyway? Lisa, you're too busy with the restaurant, even in the off-season. And Angie has flights at all hours. Chloe, how are your online classes going?"

Chloe shrugged. "They are good. I've got a pretty loyal following on social media. People love to see what I cook at the bed-and-breakfast each day. I actually went to Chicago last week for a partnership with Raven Foods."

Her friends gave suitably impressed faces that made Chloe fill with pride. "Teaching the classes is fun, but I'm glad I only do them during the off-season. Having guests every night this week at the inn means I haven't prepped for tomorrow's class yet." She winced at the thought of everything she had to do to prepare.

"Oh, that's right. That resort guy is staying at the inn. Is that weird for you? Does he know that you're the one passing out signs and rallying the whole town against him?"

Chloe shifted in her seat, suddenly uncomfortable. "I haven't turned the *whole* town against him," she murmured.

Lisa was still talking though. "I just don't know what he was thinking. This place isn't built for tourists in the winter."

"Sometimes it feels like it is barely built for tourists in the summer," Angelica joked. "Between the ferry and the no vehicles in town thing… We don't exactly make it easy for people."

Chloe laughed, remembering her own first time. "That's for sure. I don't think I had walked so much in my entire life as I did the first summer I was here. But it's kind of nice, isn't it? No cars to dodge when you walk around the square? No horns honking or exhaust fumes. On late nights, you can actually hear the insects. It wasn't even fun to walk around in Chicago in the summer because of all the heat and noise."

"Mainland pace," Angelica said with a shake of her head. The refrain was a common one around the island. Once you experienced the slow, relaxed life on the island, the craziness of other places was almost bewildering.

"It is nice. I wouldn't want to live anywhere else," Jo

admitted. "Believe me, when I got pregnant with Sam, I certainly considered it. But this is home."

"What about you, Angie? Did you ever consider moving somewhere else?" Chloe asked.

The pilot shook her head. "Nope. My brother was a little more restless," she said wistfully. Angie didn't talk about her brother much, but Chloe knew he had died many years ago in some sort of hiking accident. Angie shook her head, as though dismissing the memories. "After I moved in with Rummy and made a home on the island, I never wanted anything more than to stay here and take over Uncle Rummy's place. Which, by the way, might actually be happening sometime soon. He's been talking more and more about retiring. I think seeing Paul enjoying his free time is making my uncle think about what it would be like."

"That's so exciting. Are you ready for that? Owning a business isn't for the weak at heart," Lisa said. She would definitely know, as the owner of the Fresh Catch.

"I'm more than ready," Angelica admitted.

"Do you think that man will actually get his resort built here?" Jo asked Chloe, bringing the conversation to the original topic.

Chloe shrugged. "I don't know. The SICAB meeting got postponed." She chewed her lower lip, debating how much to share with these women. "I have a bit of a dilemma, actually."

Eyebrows lifted around the room, and her friends leaned in, obviously interested in what she was going to say. She pressed her lips together, building the tension along with her courage.

"Derrick Webster is my ex-fiancé," she blurted out, closing her eyes. "And I think I might be falling for him again, even though he's trying to ruin this town with his big fancy resort." She opened one eye, taking in the shocked expressions of her friends.

Angie let out a low whistle. "Whoa."

Chloe nodded, letting the silence settle over the room.

Lisa reached for a cookie. "We're going to need more than that. So much more, Clo."

She sighed, a laugh slipping through the breath as she pressed her hands to her face and let them muffle her words. "I know. This is crazy. I'm crazy. But he's just… He came to Bingo night, for crying out loud! And he dropped a fortune into the donation box for Bella, even though he didn't let anyone see. And he took me to The Lantern Room and set up a picnic for us after church. How do I resist that?"

"So he's falling for you too?" Angelica gasped at her next realization. "And he doesn't know that you're the protest leader?"

Chloe groaned. "Well, he knows about the signs and how I feel about the resort."

"Oh, good. I was afraid you were hiding it," Angie said.

Chloe winced. "He doesn't know that I'm on SICAB."

Lisa choked on her cookie. "Seriously? Oh, Chloe. That man has been meeting all over town with members of the board, making his pitch for the resort. How does he not know that you're on the board?"

Chloe shook her head. "I'm not sure. I think Julie hasn't updated the website yet or something."

"What are you going to do?" The soft, thoughtful question came from Jo.

"I don't know… I was going to come clean to him before the SICAB meeting yesterday morning, but then it was postponed and we were talking and I just… couldn't."

"Girl, you have to tell him!" Lisa exclaimed.

"I know… It's going to change things. And I kind of like where they are now, you know? He's… different than he used to be."

"You love him," Angelica declared, leaning back on the sofa with a smug look.

Chloe immediately shook her head. "What? No, I–"

She stopped, the words catching in her throat. Did she? Was that why she was so torn up over letting him know about her role in the future of his resort? Or why she was actually considering supporting his Family Adventure Resort when every bone in her body should keep fighting for the safe haven that was Sanctuary Island.

"There it is," Lisa said with a cackle. "Light bulb!"

"I can't love him… He's–"

"Handsome," Lisa said with an eyebrow wiggle.

"Rich," Jo added.

"Generous," Angelica said, pointing her finger toward Chloe, reminding her of the stealthy donation he'd made at Bingo night. And the Harvest of Hope Gala.

Lisa and Jo chimed in again.

"He's pretty funny."

"And ambitious."

Chloe held up her hands to the onslaught of adjectives from her friends. "Okay, okay. I get it. But he's also my ex. He chose work over our relationship over and over again. He's the reason I left Chicago and moved here. He broke my heart, guys!" She leaned back against the couch, melting into the cushion. "What am I going to do?"

She had to tell Derrick the truth about her membership in SICAB. And then, she really had to figure out which way she was going to vote. And perhaps most importantly, she had to figure out what she was going to do about these feelings for Derrick, because it didn't seem like they were going away anytime soon.

"For tonight? Just hang out with us and watch a movie. What are we watching anyway?" Angelica asked.

Lisa perked up. "Ooh, did you see Beckett Knox has a new one? Let's watch that!"

"Ooh, okay," Chloe said. "He's my favorite. I love that he insists that all his movies are faith-based. Not to mention, he's gorgeous."

Jo let out a scoff.

Chloe raised her eyebrows. "You don't think he's good-looking? Do you need your eyes checked?"

Jo shook her head. "I'll watch anything but a Beckett Knox movie. Did you know he was from here, Chloe?"

Chloe's eyes widened. "What? No! Seriously?" She looked at Lisa and Angie for confirmation. "How did I not know this?"

Jo shrugged. "Doesn't matter. At least he's gone now. The guy was a total jerk."

Lisa pressed her lips together. "People can change, Jo." Her words were gentle, contrasting Jo's vehement declaration about the celebrity.

"Maybe people can. But Beckett Knox hasn't," Jo stated firmly.

Her angry words hung in the air for a moment before Chloe spoke up, navigating the menu to a different movie. "So, *A Firefighter for Christmas* then?"

twenty-three

DERRICK

Derrick sat at a corner table in the mayor's office, the sunlight streaming through the large windows highlighting the dust motes dancing in the air. Last time he was here, he'd been too preoccupied with the discussion to notice the rest of the room. The office was furnished with an eclectic mix of historical pieces and modern instruments, a testament to Sanctuary Island's blend of old-world charm and contemporary aspirations.

Derrick was still reeling from the canceled SICAB meeting, the carpet pulled from under him while protestors still occupied the steps of Town Hall. The lukewarm reception had been a blow, but he wasn't ready to give up. He needed to secure a follow-up meeting with SICAB and get the mayor on his side.

He already felt like perhaps he had an ally in Paul

Solheim. Their impromptu chat at the coffee shop had gone better than he had hoped. Derrick had laid out his vision, emphasizing the benefits for the local economy and the job opportunities it would create. Paul had listened intently, nodding occasionally, his eyes thoughtful.

But it was when the conversation shifted to more personal topics that Derrick felt a deeper connection forming. Paul had shared stories of his own business ventures, the challenges he had faced, and the lessons he had learned along the way. He spoke of the importance of integrity and staying true to one's values, no matter the pressure to compromise.

"Success isn't only about profit, Derrick," Paul had said, his voice steady and wise. "It's about making a positive impact on the people around you. Business can be a force for good if we let it."

Derrick had nodded, absorbing Paul's words. There was something profoundly reassuring about Paul's perspective, a reminder that he could pursue his ambitions without losing sight of what truly mattered. No one in his sphere seemed to think about business in that way. Certainly not his uncle or the board of directors. The conversation had then turned to faith, and Paul had spoken of his belief in God's timing and guidance, echoing the sermon Derrick had heard at church.

"I hope you can trust in God's plan, Derrick," Paul

had advised, his eyes kind. "Sometimes, things don't happen the way we expect, but there's always a reason."

Family had been the final topic they discussed. Paul had spoken with deep affection about his wife, children, and grandchildren, emphasizing the importance of those relationships in his life. Derrick had felt a pang of longing as he listened, thinking of his own fractured family and the closeness he had once shared with Chloe.

"Family keeps us grounded," Paul had said. "They remind us of who we are and what's truly important. Never lose sight of that."

As Derrick replayed the conversation in his mind, he felt a sense of gratitude for Paul's wisdom. Here was a man who had successfully navigated the complexities of business while maintaining his integrity and nurturing his family. Paul was a role model, someone Derrick already admired deeply, despite knowing him for a short time. He was slowly realizing that someone like that had been missing for a long time. Ever since his father died, in fact.

Mayor DeBruin entered the room with a brisk stride. He extended his hand to Derrick. "Mr. Webster, good to see you."

Derrick stood to shake his hand, offering a polite smile. "You too, Mr. Mayor. How are things at the airport? Was anyone hurt?"

"Call me Jimmy, Mr. Webster," he insisted.

Derrick acknowledged the request with a nod and an invitation to call him by his first name as well.

"Thankfully no one was hurt," the mayor stated. "It was quite the fire, but they got everything under control. I'm glad Chief Warren had done so much work with the airport on protocols. We'd be in a real pickle if the airport was out of commission for any length of time."

Derrick nodded, understanding the way the island relied on the air traffic for most things during the winter.

They both sat down, and the mayor gestured for Derrick to speak first. He took a deep breath, gathering his thoughts. "As you know, the town hall meeting didn't go as well as I'd hoped. There were concerns about the resort's impact on local businesses and the community's character. I understand those concerns, and I am eager to address them with SICAB."

Jimmy nodded, his expression neutral. "The community is protective of its heritage, Derrick. They're worried about losing what makes Sanctuary Island unique."

Derrick leaned forward, his voice earnest. "I get that, and I respect it. But this resort can bring a lot of good to the island—jobs, tourism, and revenue that can be reinvested into preserving the island's charm. I'm hoping we can reschedule the meeting with SICAB as soon as possible, so we can present a revised proposal and address these concerns head-on."

"Why the rush?"

Derrick took a deep breath, deciding to be as transparent as possible. "Time is a factor because of investor commitments and seasonal considerations. We need to start construction soon to open by next summer. With winter construction challenges, delays could jeopardize the entire project."

Jimmy's expression softened slightly. "I understand. Just make sure you're prepared for the meeting. The board will need convincing, and you'll have to address every concern raised."

"I will," Derrick assured him. "I'm committed to making this work for everyone."

"Between the town hall meeting, all the signs around town, and the protestors the other morning, I think you've got your work cut out for you."

"Absolutely," Derrick agreed, knowing the mayor only spoke the truth.

Jimmy stood up and walked over to a calendar on the wall. "I can schedule you for a meeting Monday morning at 10 AM. Does that work for you?"

It was already Thursday, so a couple of days wasn't a terrible wait. "That's great. I appreciate it."

As the mayor jotted down the details, Julie, the

mayor's administrator, walked in with a file in hand. "Here are the documents you requested, Jimmy."

She turned to Derrick, her eyes sparkling with interest. "Mr. Webster, it's always a pleasure to see you."

Derrick forced a polite smile. "Likewise."

Julie lingered, her gaze lingering on Derrick longer than necessary. "If you need any help with preparations for the SICAB meeting, feel free to reach out. I'm always available."

"Thank you," Derrick said, keeping his tone professional. "I'll keep that in mind."

They discussed a few more details before Derrick took his leave. As he walked back through the town, he saw more protest signs in shop windows. His heart sank a little each time he saw another one. The message was clear: the community was not on his side.

But he wasn't ready to give up. Derrick's mind was racing with ideas for the SICAB meeting. He needed to find a way to turn the tide, to show the islanders that his resort could coexist with their way of life.

His phone rang and he paused on the sidewalk to answer it. "Webster," he said.

"Derrick, it's Harold. Just checking in. It seems as though you've all but disappeared, hiding on that same island your father used to disappear to."

Derrick clenched his jaw at the way the man's words dripped with disdain as Harold mentioned his father. It was no secret that Harold had been gunning for the Director of the Board position when his father died. Well, he could pry it from Derrick's cold, dead fingers.

"Not hiding, working. What can I do for you?" He needed to get off the phone with this man. It was seriously messing with the peaceful feeling he usually had on the island.

"I wanted to remind you of our upcoming quarterly board meeting."

"Oh wow. Are you my new assistant? I wasn't aware you'd been given a promotion."

He could actually hear the sneer on Harold's face through the phone. "You've got one more week to convince your pals on the island to give you the green light, or I'll have no trouble at all convincing the board that you're unfit for your position. You might be the heir to Webster Hotels, but we're a publicly traded company, and nothing spooks shareholders more than a lack of confidence in the man steering the ship."

Anger and frustration crashed over Derrick in waves. He tipped his head back and was greeted with a cloudy sky as he formulated his words. "I can tell you that you'll never take Webster Hotels from me. Don't forget, I'm still the majority shareholder. And that isn't going to change any time soon. If I want to spend all my time scouting out locations for future projects, then the board is going to deal with it. If I want to invest thirty million dollars into a family-friendly resort on a mostly-unknown island, then that's what we'll do. I'm in the driver's seat, Mr. Masters."

"For now," Harold replied tightly. "Enjoy your vacation, Mr. Webster."

The call disconnected and Derrick shoved his phone back in his pocket. Vacation, hah. Every minute of this trip had felt like a battle. Well, except for the time he'd spent with Chloe recently. When he first arrived, though, every encounter with her had left him battered too.

He stopped at Eastside Café to grab a coffee, his thoughts still swirling. As he waited in line, he couldn't help but think about Chloe. He was desperate to win her back, despite their differences. Would moving forward with his resort be the final nail in the coffin for them? He couldn't let that happen. With his coffee in hand, Derrick made his way back to the inn, determined to prepare for the upcoming meeting. He knew it wouldn't be easy, but he was ready to fight for his vision.

And with Paul Solheim's words in his ear, he was prepared to fight for her, too.

twenty-four

CHLOE

WITH A LAUGH, CHLOE SNAPPED A PICTURE OF DERRICK on the platform. His hand extended to clutch the fishing line that made it look as though he'd caught the giant rainbow trout in front of Fresh Catch. It was easily four feet long and as big around as her.

"When the resort gets approved, *that's* the photo I want in the paper with the announcement," he declared as she showed him the image.

"Ah, yes. Nothing says successful businessman like a cheesy tourist photo op."

He was certainly feeling confident after his meeting with the mayor earlier that day. "Exactly," he confirmed with a grin.

Her heart did backflips in her chest. Why did he have to be so charming? And why was it so hard to tell him the truth?

For the last week, it had been pretty much the only thing on her mind. But every time she thought about it, the words caught in her throat. It would only ruin things between them. Instead, every time Derrick reached for her hand, she took it and tried to memorize the feel of it, knowing it wouldn't last.

"Maybe I need one with you in it, instead?" he said, flipping his camera around to capture both of them. He tugged her close, so both their faces fit in the small screen, then turned so the trout was behind them. She smiled at the camera, but her heart wasn't in it. When Derrick turned and pressed his lips to her temple, her eyes fluttered closed, her smile slipping.

As they were seated inside the restaurant, the air was filled with the tantalizing scent of grilled fish and garlic butter. The soft glow of sunset cast a warm light over their table, creating an intimate atmosphere in the casual restaurant. The clinking of silverware and the murmur of conversations provided quiet background noise.

Chloe's stomach churned, not from the delicious food, but from the secret she carried. She pushed a piece of crab cake around her plate, her mind racing. The meeting was in a few days, and she needed to tell Derrick about her position on SICAB. The weight of the deception was becoming unbearable, especially as their connection grew stronger.

Derrick looked up from his plate, his green eyes locking onto hers. "You've been quiet tonight," he said softly, concern evident in his voice. "Is everything okay?"

Chloe took a deep breath, steeling herself. "Derrick, there's something I need to tell you—"

Before she could finish, their server appeared with a bright smile, interrupting her. "Can I get you folks anything else? Another round of drinks, perhaps?"

Chloe forced a polite smile and shook her head. "No, thank you. We're fine for now."

As the server walked away, Chloe tried to gather her thoughts again, but the moment had been disrupted. Derrick leaned closer, his expression curious and a bit worried. "What were you going to say?"

As she opened her mouth to speak, the door swung open, and a group entered, their laughter and chatter momentarily drowning out everything else. Chloe recognized several of them as employees of the Palace, the other resort on the island. One that would probably take the biggest impact of a new development.

Chloe sighed, feeling the tension coil tighter in her chest. She glanced around the restaurant, spotting familiar faces. Lisa was busy behind the bar, and a few regulars were seated at the counter, enjoying their meals.

"Derrick, I—" she began again, but once more, she

was cut off, this time by Curtis O'Connell. He had a shock of unruly red hair and a reputation for being a bit of a troublemaker. He was also the guest relations manager at the Palace.

"Hey, Derrick!" Curtis called out loudly as he approached their table, a mischievous grin on his face. "How's the fancy resort plan coming along?"

Derrick smiled tightly, clearly annoyed by the interruption. "It's going," he replied, his tone neutral.

Curtis chuckled, clearly enjoying himself. "Good thing you've got a ringer here on SICAB, right?" He winked, oblivious to the tension that suddenly thickened the air. "I've heard some of the others aren't sure how they'll vote yet. But I bet with Chloe's help, you'll have no problem convincing the committee."

Chloe's heart plummeted. She opened her mouth to speak, but before she could, Gretta joined in the conversation, her voice loud and clear. "Hah. Chloe's the one giving everyone the protest and yard signs. There's no way she would vote for the resort. She assured me that she would fight the resort with everything she had. Isn't that right, Chloe?"

The words hung in the air like a bad smell. Derrick's eyes widened, and he slowly turned to Chloe, his expression a mix of confusion and hurt. Chloe felt her cheeks flush with heat, the room suddenly too warm and too bright.

"Is it true?" Derrick asked quietly, his voice barely above a whisper.

Chloe's throat felt dry, her words stuck. She nodded slowly, unable to meet his eyes. "Yes, it's true," she admitted, her voice trembling. "I'm a member of SICAB."

The silence that followed was deafening. Derrick leaned back in his chair, his face a mask of disbelief. "The last member. Why didn't you tell me?" he asked, his voice pained.

Chloe swallowed hard, her guilt washing over her like a tidal wave. "I wanted to," she said, her voice small. "But I didn't know how. I didn't want to hurt you or make things worse. But you've always known how I felt about the resort," she insisted.

Derrick shook his head, his expression hardening. "You should have told me from the beginning. This changes everything. I knew you disagreed with the resort, but I didn't know you were planning to torpedo my plans with the entire committee." Bitterness laced every word.

Chloe felt tears prickling at the corners of her eyes. "No, I'm not… It's not like that–"

Derrick looked away, his jaw clenched. "I need some air," he said abruptly, standing up and walking toward the door without another word.

Chloe watched him go, her heart breaking. She had

feared this moment, and now that it was here, it was even worse than she had imagined. The restaurant buzzed around her, but she felt isolated, trapped in her own bubble of regret and sorrow.

Lisa approached the table, her expression sympathetic. "You okay, hon?" she asked gently.

Chloe shook her head, unable to speak. She glanced toward the door, hoping to see Derrick coming back, but he was nowhere in sight. She took a deep breath, trying to steady herself. She had made a mess of things, and now she had to find a way to fix it, if that was even possible.

The rest of the evening passed in a blur. At some point, Curtis and Gretta left her table and returned to the group from the Palace. Chloe's mind kept replaying the moment Derrick walked out, the hurt in his eyes haunting her. She had hoped that honesty would bring them closer, but instead, it had driven a wedge between them. She couldn't shake the feeling of helplessness, knowing that her actions had caused this rift.

As she finally left the restaurant, the cool night air hit her. She wrapped her arms around herself, feeling more alone than ever. The town was quiet, the only sound the distant lapping of waves against the shore. Chloe knew she had a lot to think about, and even more to apologize for.

She made her way back home, her steps heavy with

the weight of her thoughts. She didn't know what the future held, but she knew she had to find a way to make things right with Derrick.

But could she do that without selling Sanctuary Island to the highest bidder?

twenty-five

DERRICK

The events of the previous evening played on a loop in his mind, each pass deepening the pit in his stomach. Derrick sat on the edge of his bed, staring blankly at the wall of his room at the Hummingbird and Bluebell Inn. He'd turned it over all night long, on repeat like a bad song at the mall.

Chloe had deceived him. He knew she'd been against his project, her protest signs and outbursts had never been a secret, but she had also hidden her role in SICAB from him the entire time. He didn't know which emotion was stronger–the anger at her lies or the sorrow at losing whatever it was they'd been building.

He clenched his fists, his nails digging into his palms. How could she have done this to him? After everything they had shared, every moment of vulnerability, every rekindled memory of their past, she had still chosen not to tell him. Here he was, all but in love with her again. Had it all been a charade, a carefully crafted performance to gather ammunition to tank his project?

"Was any of it real?" he muttered under his breath, his voice barely above a whisper. He stood up and began to pace the room, his mind racing. Their almost kiss, the moments of connection, the intimacy they had shared during their carriage ride and the picnic—had all of that been part of her plan?

He stopped pacing and ran a hand through his hair, taking a deep breath to steady himself. The anger surged again, hot and fierce. He felt like a fool for letting his guard down, for believing that they could rebuild what they once had. The betrayal cut deeper than any business deal ever could.

This was personal.

Doubt flooded him. Chloe had kept something huge from him, and it made him look like a fool. What would the board of directors do if they found out he was falling in love with someone who had the power to shut down the project?

It was one thing to date someone who opposed the resort as a spectator. But Chloe wasn't just on the outside of the decision. She was part of the group that held the future of Webster Hotels in her hands.

As dawn broke, Derrick knew he had to face the

day. He couldn't afford to wallow in his emotions, no matter how raw they felt. He had a project to save and a meeting to prepare for. He dressed quickly, determined to keep his focus on the task at hand. He would have to deal with Chloe later.

When he walked into the dining room for breakfast, the smell of freshly brewed coffee and bacon greeted him. The room held a handful of other guests, all chatting happily over their meals. He spotted Shaun already seated at a corner table, engrossed in his phone. Derrick took a deep breath and made his way over.

Just as he reached the table, he felt a tap on his shoulder. He turned to see Chloe standing there, a tentative smile on her face. Her eyes were filled with regret, and she looked like she hadn't slept much either.

"Derrick, can we talk?" she asked softly, her voice almost drowned out by the chatter around them.

Derrick's heart tightened, but he forced himself to stay composed. "I don't think there's anything left to say, Chloe," he replied curtly, letting his words act as an icy shield. He'd done a terrible job of protecting himself and his business the last several weeks, but that ended now.

"Please, give me a chance to explain," she pleaded, her eyes searching his.

Was she looking for sympathy? Because she wasn't going to find any.

Derrick shook his head. "I have nothing to say to you right now."

Chloe stood there for a moment, hurt flashing across her face as he turned his back on her and joined Shaun at the table.

Derrick's chest ached as he turned slightly to watch her retreat, but he couldn't let himself soften. Not yet.

Shaun looked up from his phone, sensing the tension. "Everything okay?" he asked, raising an eyebrow.

"No," Derrick replied flatly, picking up a muffin and pulling off a bite without really tasting anything. "But I'll deal with it."

They ate breakfast, and Derrick tried to ignore the perfection of the food in front of him. Somehow, he thought it might feel better if Chloe had struggled this morning, even if it meant burnt toast. But he shouldn't be surprised that breakfast was still flawless. Chloe wouldn't let emotions get in the way of her responsibility. And he couldn't either.

He couldn't shake the image of her standing in the dining room, her eyes pleading for a chance to explain. Part of him wanted to hear her out, to understand her side of the story. But the pain of her betrayal was still too fresh, too raw.

For now, he would keep his distance from Chloe and focus on what needed to be done. The project was too important to let personal emotions interfere. But deep down, Derrick knew that resolving things with Chloe was just as crucial to finding any semblance of peace on this island.

Derrick's mind was still racing with thoughts of Chloe as he reviewed the documents in his room. His phone buzzed, breaking his concentration. It was Shaun, asking him to meet in the lobby. Derrick sighed, rubbing his temples once more before heading down.

Shaun was waiting, phone in hand. "We finally got a meeting with Rick Bastida. He's the SICAB member who is a general contractor. We're meeting him and Solheim in fifteen minutes at Eastside."

Derrick nodded, grateful for Shaun who was keeping things moving, despite Derrick's desire to crawl into bed until next week.

It was a short walk to the restaurant, and the sun was far too cheery for Derrick's surly mood. Paul greeted Derrick with a firm handshake and a warm smile. "Derrick, good to see you," Paul said. "This is Rick Bastida, another member of SICAB and a good friend of mine."

"Nice to meet you, Rick." The man appeared to be a few years older than Derrick, his dark features revealing his Latin heritage as much as his name.

"Likewise," he said.

Paul gestured to the chairs at the small table. "Shaun tells me you've had quite an exciting few days."

"That's one way to put it," Derrick replied, trying to muster a smile. He turned the conversation toward business, not wanting to talk about the way the betrayal still stung. "I hear you're the man to talk to about construction on the island these days, Mr. Bastida."

A small smile crossed the man's face. He gave a side-long glance to Paul. "Only because this guy over here insisted on retiring."

Derrick shook his head, an amused smile on his lips. "The audacity." He chuckled. The others joined.

Rick clapped Paul on the shoulder. "Right? No one knows construction on the island like Paul here. Actually, most of my work is on the mainland."

Derrick sighed, steepling his fingers under his chin. "Can I get your honest opinions? This resort I have planned… It's a good business decision for Webster. It's the kind of project I can get behind. And it's been a dream of mine for a long time. But am I making a mistake?"

Paul and Rick looked at each other. Silence hung in the air for what seemed like forever. It was Paul who finally broke it. "I'm happy to give you my thoughts… but I want to know something first."

"Yeah, whatever you need to know."

"Why exactly has it been a dream of yours?"

Derrick leaned back in his chair, inhaling deeply. Perhaps he shouldn't have admitted that much to these men. It could get back to the board of directors at Webster, but at this point, he didn't know what else to do.

"Every summer growing up, my parents brought me to Sanctuary Island." There were surprised looks from everyone at the table, except for Shaun. Derrick would have to evaluate that further later.

"We stayed at the Palace, hiked Seven Pines, went fishing and ate a year's worth of ice cream in a single month." He smiled at the memories as they flashed. "It was the one time of year my parents weren't completely distracted by work or society events. It was the one time we felt like a family. But it wasn't all amazing. The Palace wasn't exactly built for rambunctious eight-year-old boys. I remember breaking a huge vase in the lobby when I threw my frisbee to my dad. He wasn't paying attention to me. But the sound of shattering porcelain certainly got his attention," he said with a wistful chuckle.

"Still, all my happy memories as a kid revolve around this island. So, when market research revealed a gap in the market for family-centered resorts, I immediately thought about putting one here. Even more so when the market research team had Sanctuary Island listed as their number one recommended destination.

Coming during the off-season reinforced my desire to help by creating an attraction that would benefit the island year-round."

He met the eyes of the men across the table again. "My board isn't sold on the idea of family resorts. And they definitely don't think I'm qualified to lead the charge, seeing as I basically ignored my fiancée and threw away the only chance I had for real love and real family since my parents died." Who was he to spearhead a project about family when he barely seemed to know the meaning of the word?

"Are you? Qualified, I mean? Has anything changed in that regard?" The poignant question came from Rick.

Derrick exhaled. "I would have said yes a few weeks ago. Tried to sell you on all my qualifications and business acumen. But now... I don't know. Chloe and I..."

"Wait... Chloe?" Paul asked with a raised eyebrow.

"Oh... didn't I tell you that part?" Derrick heard the cynicism in his own voice. "Chloe is the aforementioned ex-fiancée. And ever since I got here, I haven't done anything except alienate her even more, despite wanting to win her back with every fiber of my being. So, what do I know about family?" His words were laced with bitterness, and he stared into the dark depths of his coffee.

Shaun spoke up for the first time in the meeting. "So let me get this straight. You come to Sanctuary to build this big family resort and discover that your ex-fiancée has since moved here and become a beloved part of the community. She opposes you with every ounce of energy she has, and you keep pursuing her heart as well as the resort. Then you find out that she's on the committee that has the power to kill the project and didn't tell you."

Derrick nodded. "Yeah, that pretty much sums it up." His frustration and anger resurfaced. "I feel betrayed. She kept this from me, and I'm sort of worried our entire relationship was a ploy. So yeah, you're right." He pressed his hands to his face. "Except you missed the part where I'm tempted to torpedo the whole project myself if it meant she'd give me a second chance, even though it probably means I'd end up with a vote of no confidence from the board at Webster. But I'm terrified that she'd still hate me, and then I'd be left with no job as well as no Chloe."

Rick gave a low whistle. "No wonder you're wound tighter than the winch crank on a full net."

The description was so colorful and spot-on that Derrick's wry laughter escaped before he could stop it. "You could definitely say that." He glanced up at Paul, interested to see what the man thought of his confessions. Paul was quiet, and Derrick couldn't read his face.

When Derrick finished, Paul leaned forward, his

eyes piercing. "Derrick, I understand your anger. But let me ask you something—what is it that you're really angry about?

Derrick blinked, caught off-guard by the question. "I'm angry that she lied to me, that she's been using my feelings for me to soften me up, just to work against me this whole time." At least that was the worst-case scenario.

"Or... Are you angry because you care about her?" Paul challenged gently. "Because you thought you were rebuilding something special, only to remember that she's on the other side of this issue?"

Derrick opened his mouth to respond, but the words caught in his throat. Paul continued, his voice calm and steady. "Derrick, I've been on this island my whole life. I've seen it change, grow, and face challenges. Sanctuary is a special place, and it's no wonder Chloe wants to protect it. The question you need to ask yourself is—what do you want?"

Derrick stared at Paul, the older man's wisdom cutting through his anger. What did he want? To build the resort, yes. But more than that, he wanted a future, one that increasingly included Chloe.

"If you're serious about building a life with Chloe, you'll need to find a way to understand her perspective, to forgive her," Paul said, leaning back. "Sanctuary isn't just a project. Or a memory. It's a community, a home.

And if you love it as much as you say, you'll need to show it. And you should remember who Chloe is. Because there's no way she would have pretended to care about you in order to ruin your project."

"That's true," Shaun added with a grin. "She was perfectly happy trying to publicly derail the project while she still hated you."

"So helpful, Shaun," he said with sarcasm.

Chloe's passion for Sanctuary was one of the things he admired most about her. Her love for the island was not unlike his own, and in many ways, it mirrored his reasons for wanting to build something meaningful here. His anger began to dissolve, replaced by a deep, aching understanding.

"Paul, you're right," Derrick admitted, his voice softer. "I've been so focused on the project that I forgot why I loved coming here in the first place. I want to be part of this community, to create something lasting. And I can't do that by being angry with Chloe for loving this place."

Paul smiled, nodding. "Sanctuary has a way of bringing out the best in people. It challenges you to look beyond yourself. If you can do that, Derrick, you'll find a way to make this work. And," he said with a smile, "I think I might have an idea for how to do it."

twenty-six

CHLOE

THE REGRET AND DISAPPOINTMENT SAT LIKE A WEIGHT IN her gut as Chloe stood outside town hall. The morning sun was casting long shadows across the cobblestone square. She had arrived early, hoping to gather her thoughts before the crucial SICAB meeting. Her mind raced with memories of the past few days—Derrick's anger, his vulnerability, and the deep, unresolved feelings that lingered between them. He had every right to be angry with her for keeping her membership a secret.

But she'd never pretended she would do anything except stand up for Sanctuary Island. And that was what she was going to do today. If Derrick chose business over her again, then she would have to find a way to survive it—again. This was exactly why she shouldn't have gotten so involved with him in the first place.

But she couldn't entirely regret the mistakes. She finally had some closure about their relationship that had ended six years ago. And she no longer saw Derrick as the villain in her story.

When you knew the shades of gray behind someone's actions, it was much harder to view their choices in black and white. Knowing the pressure he was under to perform for Webster Hotels didn't make the choices he'd made right. But it gave her some context to give him more grace.

She took a deep breath and walked inside, finding her seat at the long conference table. The other board members slowly filled the room, each person representing a piece of Sanctuary's close-knit community. Chloe's eyes never left the door, her heart pounding in anticipation while she waited for Derrick.

He strode into the room, Shaun on his heels. While she felt like she hadn't slept in days, Derrick was the very picture of a confident businessman. His suit was neatly pressed, and his green tie nearly matched the color of his eyes.

He stood near the front, talking quietly with Shaun, his expression serious yet determined.

"Good morning, everyone," the mayor began. "We're here today to discuss a proposal for a new business on Sanctuary Island. Mr. Derrick Webster will present his plans. Afterward, we'll open the floor for questions and then proceed to our vote."

Derrick stepped up to the podium, his eyes briefly meeting Chloe's. He took a deep breath, looking around the room with a confident smile. "Thank you, Mr. Mayor. Good morning, everyone. I want to start by acknowledging a few things first. Sanctuary is a special place, and I understand why so many of you are protective of it."

He clicked the remote in his hand, and a projection screen behind him lit up with images of the island's natural beauty—the lush forests, the serene lake, the charming town square.

"I came to Sanctuary with a vision for a large resort that would meet our guests' every need. I wanted to bring as many people to the island as I could. But, by showing me the heart behind Sanctuary, someone very special helped me realize that wasn't what the island really needs. And it wouldn't provide my guests with the experience I remember from the five summers I spent here as a child."

There were a few murmurs and raised eyebrows at his announcement. Derrick had been so careful not to let anyone know that he had a personal connection to the island. So why was he sharing it now?

"Over the past few weeks, I've come to see this

island through your eyes. It's not just a place; it's a home, a community, a sanctuary in every sense of the word. When I was here as a child, the summers meant a break from the busyness of daily life. A chance for my family to reconnect and a place to build memories. It was ice cream at The Pearl and hikes through Seven Pines. It was biking everywhere instead of having our driver pick us up at the door. It was fishing off the pier and skipping rocks into the water. That's what I want for the families who visit the Family Adventure Resort. I want them to come, connect, and appreciate everything Sanctuary Island has to offer—not just the inside of my resort."

Chloe's breath caught as she listened. There was something different about Derrick today—his tone, his approach. It was as if he were speaking directly to her, trying to bridge the gap that had formed between them.

Derrick continued, his voice steady. "What Sanctuary needs during the off-season is something that complements its charm, not changes it." His eyes met hers and held them. "I'm done missing out on things that are perfect the way they are, because of my own misunderstanding of success."

Her breath caught. It almost sounded like…

He clicked the remote again, and new images appeared. They were just concept sketches. A much smaller resort, nestled into the landscape with minimal disruption. "This is my revised proposal. This boutique resort has fewer rooms, designed to blend seamlessly with the environment. The wood-and-glass exterior will reflect the water and complement the trees. We'll use local materials and labor. And instead of building amenities that would compete with local businesses, we'll partner with them. Guests will be encouraged to dine at our local restaurants, shop in our stores, and experience everything our island has to offer."

Chloe's heart stuttered at the way he referred to Sanctuary as "our" island.

The room was silent, the weight of Derrick's words hanging in the air. Chloe felt a swell of pride mixed with confusion. This wasn't the plan they had fought over. This was something different, something that respected the island's unique character.

"As part of this proposal," Derrick continued, "the resort will also have a community coalition, made up of local residents and business owners, to ensure that the resort remains aligned with Sanctuary's values. We'll have a concierge service that recommends local restaurants, shops, and activities. We'll also host events that bring guests into town, creating more foot traffic and opportunities for everyone. This isn't just my project; it's ours. Together, we can create something that benefits everyone."

Chloe's heart ached as she listened. Derrick was

trying so hard to make things right, to show that he understood what Sanctuary meant to her and to everyone else. Derrick wrapped up his presentation, looking around the room with a hopeful smile. "Thank you for your time. I'm here to answer any questions you may have."

Mayor DeBruin nodded and opened the floor for questions. Hands shot up, and Derrick fielded each one with patience. He explained the steps he would take to involve the community in every stage of the project, the amenities the resort would include, the number of jobs the resort would create, and how they would tackle the logistics of winter weather and lack of ferry during the off-season.

Chloe listened intently, her emotions in turmoil. Derrick's answers were sincere, his plan thoughtful and considerate. She couldn't help but feel a flicker of hope. Maybe they could find a way to make this work.

The mayor called for a short break before the board's private deliberation and vote. Derrick stepped down from the podium, his eyes seeking Chloe's. She stood up and walked over to him, her heart pounding. Several other board members reached him first, and he exchanged polite words with them before finally turning to her.

"Derrick," she began, her voice trembling slightly. "You've really thought this through."

He smiled, the warmth in his eyes melting some of the ice that had formed between them. “Thank you. I meant every word. I want this to work, for all of us. I wanted to talk to you before, but–”

The mayor yelled for attention and called the meeting to order. “We’ve heard Mr. Webster’s revised proposal. Now, it’s time for us to discuss and vote. Privately,” he added with a glance at Derrick.

“Thank you, sir,” he said to the mayor. Then, Derrick squeezed her hands. “Whatever happens, I want you to know that I care about Sanctuary, and I care about you.”

Chloe’s heart ached at his words. She wanted to believe him, to trust that he had changed. But the wounds from their past were still fresh, and the stakes were so high. “I’ll see you after the vote,” she whispered, tugging her hands away.

He nodded, giving her a small, hopeful smile before turning to leave the room. Chloe watched him go, her mind racing. She was proud of him, of the way he had listened and adapted. But she was also scared. Scared of getting hurt again, scared of making the wrong decision.

As the board reconvened, Chloe took her seat, her heart heavy with uncertainty. Chloe listened as her fellow board members voiced their opinions. Some were skeptical, others cautiously optimistic.

The weight of her decision pressed down on her. The vote was called, and one by one, the board members cast their ballots. Chloe's heart pounded as the final votes were tallied.

twenty-seven

DERRICK

DERRICK PACED THE LENGTH OF THE MAYOR'S OFFICE, THE tension in his shoulders unrelenting. The mahogany furniture, adorned with polished brass fixtures, seemed to gleam with an almost oppressive shine in the midday light streaming through the large windows. Derrick paused by a bookshelf, running his fingers along the spines of various historical tomes and local records. Shaun was there too, his fingers glued to his phone keyboard.

Derrick groaned again and resumed his pacing. "What is taking so long?"

Shaun barely glanced up. "I'd tell you to chill out, but I think that would be pointless."

He tugged on his tie, tired of feeling like he was being strangled. "Probably," he admitted. Without a doubt, he was going to be on edge until he could talk to Chloe. His steps faltered.

Was he nervous about the vote? Or about the conversation he needed to have with Chloe?

He'd assumed it was the first, but examining the thoughts that had been swirling in his mind since he left the conference room, they all centered around Chloe and the interrupted conversation. He was desperate to know what she'd thought of his new plan. He'd spent two days non-stop working on it after the meeting with Paul. He hadn't even come down for breakfast, insisting on having it sent to his room instead. But as he'd worked on the proposal, every decision had been weighed against what Chloe would approve of.

He was expecting the mayor any minute to inform him of the board's final decision. He took a seat in one of the plush leather chairs, trying to calm his racing thoughts. He had repeatedly zeroed in on Chloe's expression as she had listened to him present his revised plans. There had been hope in her eyes that had made his heart ache with anticipation. But there had also been hesitation in her gaze, and he was desperately afraid that those reservations would win.

The door creaked open, and Derrick looked up, expecting to see the mayor. Instead, Chloe stepped in, closing the door softly behind her. She looked slightly nervous, her hands clasped in front of her, but there was a determined glint in her eyes.

"Chloe," he said, standing up, his heart leaping at the sight of her. "I thought the mayor was coming to give me the news."

"He was," Chloe replied, her voice steady despite the slight tremor Derrick could see in her hands. "But I asked if I could break the news instead."

Derrick's breath caught, his heart sinking to the floor. "Just tell me," he pleaded.

Chloe took a step closer, her eyes never leaving his. "The board has agreed to move forward with your revised plans. There are still conditions and oversight, but they've approved it."

Relief washed over Derrick, but it was quickly replaced by a myriad of other emotions—gratitude, hope, and the unresolved feelings that had been simmering between them for weeks. "I'm really glad they're giving this a chance." He reached out and tucked a stray lock of hair behind her ear, his touch gentle and tender. "And what about you?"

There was a sadness in her eyes that tugged at Derrick's heart. "There's so much history here, and not just with the island."

"That's my cue to leave," Shaun said with barely disguised glee, slipping out the door and leaving them alone.

Derrick took a deep breath, stepping closer to her. "I've been thinking a lot about that—about us. The past few weeks have made me realize how much I've missed you, and how much I regret the choices I made."

Chloe's eyes softened, but she didn't say anything, waiting for him to continue.

"I was so focused on my career, on meeting the expectations of everyone around me, that I lost sight of what really mattered," Derrick said, his voice raw with emotion. "You."

Tears welled up in Chloe's eyes, and she blinked them back, her breath hitching. "I was so angry with you, for so long. And when I finally thought I'd moved on... you showed up and blew that whole idea to pieces. I didn't want to... but you made me remember why I fell in love with you in the first place."

Derrick sucked in a breath. Did that mean–

"What if... what if I'm still not enough for you?"

The words pierced whatever was left of the flimsy armor he'd worn when he arrived on the island. "Oh, Saucy. You were always enough. Can't you see that? As much as I wanted to blame you for leaving, the truth was that I chased you away." Derrick's heart pounded in his chest. "I never stopped loving you, Chloe. And I don't want to lose you again."

Chloe closed the remaining distance between them, her hands reaching up to cup his face. "I don't want to lose you either," she whispered. "I'm afraid. What if you choose work over me again?" The world seemed to stop as they stood there.

Derrick leaned into the contact, his forehead resting against hers, their breaths mingling in the space between them. "I have a memo waiting to be signed to the board of directors, canceling everything on the plans for the resort here. I know the committee approved it, but if you don't want me to build here, I choose you. Every time. I want you to know that I wouldn't make that same choice today. Not knowing what it cost me six years ago."

The years since he found that ring on the kitchen counter stretched out behind him, endless moments they missed because of his own stubbornness and pride. No, he'd never choose work over Chloe again.

"Chloe," he murmured, his voice barely a whisper. "I love you."

"I love you too," she replied, her voice trembling with emotion. "And I voted yes."

His heart went into overdrive with her admission, a smile spreading across his lips in victory. Ever since he'd set foot on this island, he'd been fighting for his resort. But maybe, in reality, he'd been fighting for something far more important.

He'd been fighting for her heart.

Something he should have done six years ago but

had been too hurt to do. Too scared. Too insecure about his place at Webster Hotels to fight for the life he deserved outside of the boardroom.

As much as he wanted to make his parents proud, he knew that it was this decision that they would have approved of.

Finally, he pressed his lips to Chloe's, sliding his hand under her jaw, the delicate skin as soft as spun silk. He kissed her gently at first, afraid of shattering the fragile hope that blossomed between them. "You're so perfect," he whispered against her lips, covering her denial with his mouth. He poured years of longing and unspoken words into that one, perfect moment where she was finally his again.

Derrick's arms wrapped around Chloe, pulling her closer, and she melted into his embrace, her fingers tangling in his hair. A rumble of satisfaction vibrated in his chest as he savored the contact. Everything about this woman drove him absolutely crazy. Her passion and her loyalty to this community. Her taste, her sweetness, and every curvy inch of her body all called to him like a siren, luring him to his downfall. But she wasn't his downfall. She was his future.

He wanted Chloe to be his. Forever.

His hands found the small of her back, every inch of her pressed against him as he held her desperately. Her nearness was a heady dose of bliss that had his mind spiraling. He'd never admit it to anyone, but she'd all but destroyed him by leaving once, and he'd make sure she never felt the need to do so again. He'd give her the whole world if it meant more moments like this one. The kiss was everything he had remembered and more —a promise of forgiveness, of new beginnings, of a love that had never truly faded. It was familiar and entirely different at the same time.

When they finally pulled back, they were both breathless, their foreheads still touching as they gasped for air. Chloe smiled up at him, her eyes shining with happiness. "So, what now?"

Derrick chuckled softly, brushing a strand of hair away from her face. He had been given a second chance, and he wasn't going to waste it.

"Now, we build something together. For the island, and for us."

Chloe nodded, her smile widening. "I'd like that."

twenty-eight

CHLOE

CHLOE WALKED BESIDE DERRICK AS THEY LEFT THE mayor's office, their hands entwined. Chloe felt as if she were walking on air. She glanced at Derrick, his profile strong and confident, and felt a surge of affection alongside hope for the future. She still couldn't believe he had completely redesigned the resort.

As they passed Eastside Café, Winona was outside pulling dead plants from the window boxes. She did a double take when she saw them, and her gaze locked on their joined hands.

"Well, well. What do we have here?" Winona asked.

Chloe squirmed but squeezed Derrick's hand. "We're heading to The Bluebell. We need to celebrate the good news."

"Good news?" Winona glanced at the bright-red

sign still hanging in the window, declaring her protest of the resort.

Chloe stepped forward. "Derrick presented a completely revised resort proposal to SICAB this morning, and the board approved it."

Derrick's presentation had been nothing short of remarkable. He had focused on all the wonderful things about Sanctuary, emphasizing his desire to preserve its charm and uniqueness. His heartfelt words had resonated with everyone in the room, especially Chloe. She had been so proud of him, not just for the presentation, but for his willingness to change and adapt.

Winona's eyes widened and she looked between Chloe and Derrick again. "I can't believe you would do this to us, Chloe. I thought you were one of us. We trusted you!"

Chloe felt the sharp sting of the woman's words, as though they'd been a slap to the face. "I–I am. Sanctuary is my home."

But Winona shook her head. "You know he's only using you, right? He found out you were on the board and figured he could use a relationship to guarantee your vote. How much did it cost him? Dinner at The Lantern Room? Or was it that private flight to Chicago that did it?"

"That's enough." Derrick's commanding voice came from just behind her. "You can insult me all you want, but leave Chloe out of this. It was her compassion for and knowledge of the island that forced me to take a closer look at the impact of my resort. The entire advisory board and the mayor agreed that the solution is an excellent fit for Sanctuary and will benefit everyone. So instead of turning her into the enemy, you should be thanking her."

Winona rolled her eyes and disappeared inside the small cafe.

Chloe flushed with pleasure as Derrick defended her. She knew it would be a hard pill for some of the town to swallow. After all, she'd led the charge for the movement against the protest, but in the end, she'd voted for it.

"They approved it?"

Chloe's eyes slid to her right and found Gretta, from the Palace, had stopped in her tracks across the sidewalk.

"Gretta, I can explain–"

Gretta shook her head. "Don't bother, it's completely fine. The advisory board is in place for a reason, after all." Gretta's voice was pinched in false pleasantness. "Excuse me, I must go."

Chloe sighed as the uptight manager of the only large resort on Sanctuary Island strode away, her heels striking the brick street in a rhythmic beat.

"You okay?" Derrick said, pressing his lips to the top

of her head. His arm was around her shoulder now, pulling her close to his side.

She sighed. "Yeah, I'm okay. Everyone will be okay with it, once they know the truth."

"Which truth is that?" Derrick asked. "The one where I'm madly in love with you?"

She grinned, unable to restrain the giddiness that came with his declaration. "Well, that will probably help," she admitted. "But I was talking about the fact that you addressed every concern we had about the impact of the resort."

"Oh. I think I'd rather everyone was talking about the other thing," he said with a wink.

Chloe led him toward the back entrance of The Bluebell, pausing in front of the door and facing him, both hands in his. "What else do you have to do today?"

"Well, I have some pretty big news to share with my board of directors to get things moving on the resort. Why do you ask?"

Chloe glanced toward the door of the inn. "I've got a catering order to prepare this afternoon."

His eyebrows rose. "So, you're telling me that my girlfriend will be working down the hall from where I'll be trying to focus on my work?"

She nodded, feeling her stomach flip and her cheeks warm at being called his girlfriend.

He pressed a kiss to her lips. "Maybe I can keep you company in the kitchen?"

After a quick stop by his room, Derrick met Chloe in the kitchen. She set to work preparing her catering order. She set up her camera as well, pressing record so she could use some of this prep to make a new video. She really needed to keep her social media views up, since that was how most of her video class clients found her.

Derrick leaned back against the counter, watching her with an expression that made her heart flutter. She was acutely aware of his presence and the warmth of his gaze. The memory of their kiss was still fresh in her mind.

"So, what's on the menu tonight?" Derrick asked, his voice playful.

Chloe smiled, feeling a rush of affection. She stepped around him, reaching for the mixing bowls on the bottom rack to his left. "Well, Easter is coming up, and I've got quite a few orders for pies, dinner rolls, and my famous cheesy potatoes."

"Sounds delicious," he replied, his eyes never leaving her.

When she walked around to the other side of the counter, he followed her steps. He caged her with his arms, his front to her back and his breath tickling her neck as he kissed her gently there. She rolled her head to one side, giving him better access. "Am I distracting you?" he murmured.

"Yes," she scolded him, though not very convincingly. "Don't you have work to do?"

He nuzzled her again, the soft scruff of his stubble tickling her neck. She giggled and tried to squirm away, only to end up face-to-face with her back pressed against the counter and his eyes locked on hers. "I thought I told you I would always choose you over work."

Chloe's reply about that being entirely impractical disappeared as Derrick cupped her cheek with his hand, brushing his thumb over her lower lip ever so lightly. Then he lowered his face and captured her mouth with his. Every thought disappeared except the blissful reality of being the sole focus of this incredible man. She pressed into the kiss, eager for more, somehow still fighting him despite their battle about the resort ending. Though this time, it was a fight waged with her fists clenched in his shirt and soft sighs of pleasure.

"Am I interrupting something?"

Chloe's eyes flew open, flicking to the door to find Marissa standing there, her eyes twinkling with amusement.

Heat flushed through Chloe's entire body as she released her grip on his dress shirt. Chloe laughed, feeling the blush creep up her neck and cheeks. "Not at all," she said, gently pushing Derrick away with both arms, trying to discreetly wipe away the evidence of the kiss from her lips.

Marissa walked around to the other side of the counter. "I see things have progressed nicely between you two," she teased, a knowing smile on her face.

Derrick grinned, unabashed. "You could say that," he replied, still keeping close to Chloe. "We're celebrating."

"And what, exactly, could you be celebrating–together?" Marissa asked, though Chloe suspected she already knew the answer. Nothing stayed a secret very long on this island. Someone had probably sent live updates to the community Facebook group during the vote itself.

Chloe grinned. "Derrick's revised resort proposal was approved by the board. And by me," she added with a sheepish smile.

"So you don't hate him?"

Chloe shook her head. "I don't think I ever really did," she admitted, glancing up at Derrick, who only smiled warmly back, affection written all over his face.

"Even when you threw coffee in my face?" he said, his smile letting her know all was forgiven.

Marissa turned her gaze to Chloe. "I'm so happy for you. I knew things weren't as over as you said they were."

Chloe ducked her head, embarrassed to have Derrick aware that she'd talked to Marissa about him.

Marissa wasn't done though. She turned to Derrick. "But, Mr. Webster, I don't care who you are in the big city. You'd better not hurt her again, or you'll find out exactly how unfriendly our little island can be."

Chloe felt a pang of worry mixed with gratitude for Marissa's protective nature. She glanced at Derrick.

"So I got the *friendly* welcome wagon this time?"

Chloe laughed, remembering his first few days on the island, and exactly how unwelcoming she had been to him.

"I won't hurt her, Marissa. I promise," Derrick said earnestly, his gaze shifting to Chloe. "I know what's at stake."

Marissa nodded, satisfied. "Good. Because she deserves the best." She patted Chloe's hand affectionately. "I'll leave you two lovebirds alone."

As Marissa left the kitchen, anxiety settled over Chloe, dampening her joy from just minutes ago. She turned back to Derrick, her thoughts swirling with uncertainty about their future. "Derrick," she began, her voice tentative. "What happens now? When are you going back to Chicago?"

Derrick's face tightened. He reached for her hands, holding them gently. "Chloe, I'm not going anywhere. Even if I have to go back to the city, I'm always going to come right back. I'm going to see this project through, but even beyond that, I want to be with you."

A rush of relief mingled with her lingering doubt. "But what about your life in Chicago? Your business?"

He sighed, his thumb brushing soothing circles on the back of her hand. "I've been thinking about that a lot. My life has always been about work. I've been running myself into the ground trying to make everyone else happy. But being here with you, it's made me realize that there's so much more."

Chloe's heart swelled with hope, but she couldn't help the lingering fear. "And what if you get pulled back into that world? What if this is just a temporary escape, and after the resort is done, you–"

Derrick shook his head, his eyes serious. "It's not a temporary escape, Chloe. And if you hated my new idea for the resort, I was completely prepared to abandon the plan and do whatever it took to convince you to give me another shot. I'm committed to making this work. For us and for Sanctuary. I love this place, and I love you. I want to build a future here. All this time, I've been keeping people out–keeping *you* out–because I was afraid to let you see how broken I really am. But I think… I think I'm finding the same thing you found when you came to Sanctuary."

"And what's that?"

"That God takes our brokenness and turns it into something beautiful in His time."

She looked into his eyes, searching for any hint of doubt but finding only sincerity. "I love you too, Derrick. But I can't leave Sanctuary. This is my home. It's everything to me."

"I know," he said softly, pulling her closer. "And I don't want you to leave. I want to be part of your world, part of this community. I can run Webster Hotels from anywhere, and I think our flagship Family Adventure Resort is the absolutely perfect place for my new office."

twenty-nine
DERRICK

DERRICK STOOD AT THE EDGE OF THE CLEARED LAND, A crisp breeze ruffling his hair. It was an unseasonably warm day for late April, the sun shining brightly overhead. A month had passed since the SICAB meeting, and now they were finally breaking ground on the resort, the usually painfully slow paperwork sped along nicely by the power of his checkbook. The smell of fresh earth filled the air, mingling with the scent of blooming wildflowers from the nearby meadows.

Mayor DeBruin stood beside him. Chloe was on his other side, her presence the only thing he really needed. None of this would have happened without her. Derrick glanced at her, admiring the way her eyes sparkled in the sunlight. Julie from the mayor's office was acting as the official photographer, busy capturing the moment, ensuring this historic day would be well-documented.

Derrick cleared his throat and stepped forward, the chatter of the small crowd quickly dying. "Thank you all for being here today," he began, his voice steady and clear. "This project has been a journey, one that wouldn't have been possible without the support and guidance of this wonderful community. Our goal with this resort is not only to build something new, but to enhance what already makes Sanctuary so special. We want to honor the beauty, history, and spirit of this place."

He paused, his eyes sweeping over the familiar faces in the crowd. There was Paul Solheim, whose inspiring sermon had opened Derrick's eyes. And Marissa, who had welcomed him to the Hummingbird and Bluebell, graciously letting him stay there each time he visited Sanctuary over the last month. Which, due to the lovely woman beside him, had been far more nights than not.

Rick Bastida was there, along with Tom Fuller, the schoolteacher Derrick had since met. Elijah, Candi, and even Winona who had been so upset the day of the vote were here. It hadn't taken long for most everyone who had opposed the resort to be on board after hearing the updated proposal. And everyone seemed to appreciate that Chloe had done everything she could to protect the island every step of the way.

"I believe in this community, and I believe in what we can achieve together. Today marks the beginning of a new chapter, one that I hope will bring prosperity to Sanctuary for years to come." With that, Derrick took the ceremonial shovel and dug into the earth, lifting the first clump of soil.

The crowd erupted into applause, and Julie clicked away on her camera, capturing the triumphant moment. It had been four weeks since the SICAB meeting where everything had fallen into place, and Derrick had been pulling every string to make sure the project started without delay.

After the formalities, Derrick found Chloe, who was beaming with pride. "You did great," she said, squeezing his hand. "I'm so proud of you."

"Thanks," he replied, his heart swelling with gratitude and love. "But the day's not over yet. I have a surprise for you. You're to go with Marissa to The Bluebell and do whatever she tells you, okay?"

Curiosity sparked in her eyes as they walked toward the cars that would take them back to the edge of town. "What's all this about, Derrick?"

"You'll see. Today is really special for me and Webster Hotels, and I wanted to do something equally special for you."

Chloe looked like she had more to say, but Marissa swooped in. "Let's go, sugar. Your man has everything arranged, okay?" She led Chloe to the car and gave a wave and a wink behind her. Marissa knew exactly what Derrick had planned and had been more than happy to assist by setting up the dress and pampering for Chloe at the Bluebell.

He tried his best to work while he waited, but the hours passed painfully slowly. He was working from the rented office he'd set up in town, finding it nearly impossible to work at the inn knowing that Chloe was just down the hall. Finally, it was almost seven. He went to the inn and got ready himself.

He was waiting in the entry parlor when Marissa entered the room and nudged him toward the foyer. Like a vision from a dream, Chloe descended the stairs wrapped in the elegant satin dress he'd selected. The dark blue was stunning against her skin, bringing her blue eyes out even more. Her golden tresses trailed over her shoulders, and he felt his fingers itch to caress the skin there, too.

"Wow," he breathed. "You look… Wow."

His mind flicked back to the way his brain had short-circuited when she'd come down for their gala in Chicago. All the compliments he hadn't been able to give her that night, too caught up in his own pride, he was determined to shower her with tonight.

"I am the luckiest man in the world," he said as she crossed the room toward him.

"You look awfully nice yourself," she said. "I didn't think The Lantern Room was open tonight?"

Derrick winked at her. "You don't think I could get them to open for us?"

"He's a billionaire, Chloe," came Marissa's helpful reply.

He grinned.

Chloe rolled her eyes and groaned. "He's not a billionaire."

That was technically true, but he had a pretty good feeling that after the next annual report from Webster Hotels, he'd be able to claim that title. But for the first time, he didn't really care as much as he always had. He'd found the real treasure, and she couldn't be held in a bank account or safety deposit box.

"Come on, my love. Let's see what we have planned this evening."

Taylor picked them up in front of The Bluebell in the same small horse-drawn carriage. While tourists were beginning to arrive, it was not officially the busy season yet. Plus, Derrick had once again bribed the grumpy horseman to bend his rules.

Chloe gave a questioning look when Taylor turned the opposite direction, clearly not heading for the lighthouse. He took them to the small parking lot near the public beach, directly across from the site of the new resort.

Derrick helped Chloe down from the carriage and down the small wooden boardwalk to the sand. Derrick had arranged for a private table on the sand, set under a tent with billowing white curtains and strings of Edison bulbs casting a warm, golden glow. The sound of gentle waves lapping against the shore provided a soothing soundtrack.

As they approached, Chloe gasped. "Derrick, this is beautiful."

He smiled, feeling a surge of satisfaction. "I wanted to do something special for you."

The table was elegantly set with fine china and silverware, and the aroma of gourmet food wafted through the air. "I told you it wasn't The Lantern Room," Derrick said as he pulled out her chair. "But I did have their chef prepare our food," he added with a grin, loving the way her face transformed at the announcement.

"You're ridiculous, Derrick Webster."

The meal featured tender beef and buttery shrimp with a delicate chocolate mousse for dessert. The conversation flowed easily. As the evening grew cooler, Derrick draped his jacket over Chloe's shoulders, not wanting to see her the least bit uncomfortable. Plus, he could admit he was basically a caveman deep down, and seeing her in his clothes? Yeah, it made him want to pound his chest.

After dinner, Derrick took a deep breath, his heart pounding. This was the moment he had been planning for weeks. He reached into his pocket and pulled out a small velvet box. "Chloe, there's something I've been wanting to ask you."

Her eyes widened as he got down on one knee, opening the box to reveal her original engagement ring. "Six years ago, you left this behind. You left me behind."

Her soft murmur made him shake his head.

His faith had been tested and strengthened, and he knew that his commitment to Chloe was unwavering. He had learned the importance of forgiveness, of understanding, and of never giving up on the ones you love.

"You did the right thing. Because back then, I had no idea what I had. I thought about getting rid of it a hundred times, but I never could. Now, I have to admit that's because I had never truly moved on from you. I could never let go of the hope that we might find our way back to each other. Chloe, I'm asking again. Will you marry me?"

For a moment, she was silent, her eyes glistening with tears, frozen on the ring. Derrick's heart raced, worried that he had misjudged her feelings. "If you don't like it, we can get a new one," he stammered. "I just thought—"

"No," she interrupted, her voice choked with

emotion. She reached out and grabbed the ring, clutching it tightly. "It's mine. It's always been mine. And I've always been yours, as much as I didn't want to be."

Relief and joy washed over him as he slid the ring onto her finger. She pulled him up and kissed him, a kiss filled with all the love and promise of their future together. Derrick held her close, the world around them fading away.

As they stood there, wrapped in each other's arms, Derrick looked into Chloe's eyes, seeing their shared dreams reflected back at him. "I promise to always choose you," he whispered.

They stood there for a long time, the stars beginning to twinkle above them, the sound of the lake a gentle reminder of the vast, beautiful world they were going to explore together. But no matter where they ventured, they would always return to the place that had shaped them as individuals and as a couple. This was their home – their Sanctuary.

epilogue

CHLOE

Chloe met Angie's eyes in the mirror. "Are you sure about this, Chloe? Because if you're not, my plane is fueled up and ready to go. We can get you out of here before he knows you're gone."

Jo and Lisa were there, too, waiting for her answer.

Chloe smiled at her friends, then adjusted the comb on her netted birdcage-style veil. "I've never been more sure about anything in my life," she reassured them. She didn't need it, but knowing that they would without-a-doubt stage a full-on evacuation if she needed one was incredibly heartwarming.

They'd chosen a short engagement, Derrick insisting that he'd already wasted six years and was determined not to waste another. With how busy everyone was during the summer, it was either sneak a wedding in before Memorial Day weekend or wait until the season was over. So, pulling together a wedding in three weeks it was.

She'd flown to Chicago to buy this dress off the rack. A very expensive rack, at Derrick's insistence, but a rack nonetheless.

Jo turned around and fixed Samantha's hair. She was their flower girl and was beaming in her dress.

"Two-minute warning," came Marissa's voice from the hallway.

Chloe felt her heart suddenly kick up. She hadn't been nervous all day, but now that the moment was here? Those weren't just butterflies in her stomach. Those were seagulls or something.

"Deep breath, honey. You love him. He loves you." Lisa's unflappable calm was exactly what she needed.

She inhaled as deeply as she could and then blew it out. "I'm okay," she said, meeting their eyes in the mirror again. "Go. I'm right behind you."

Her friends filed out of the small Sunday School classroom they were using as a dressing room, and she took one last glance in the mirror before following them to the worship center.

The wedding was small, at least by billionaire standards. But it seemed that most of Sanctuary had shown up. When the music started and the doors opened though, she didn't see anyone but the man waiting at the end of the aisle.

Derrick's eyes were locked on hers, and the rest of the world melted away. Chloe's heart swelled with a love so intense it felt like it might burst from her chest. She walked slowly, deliberately, each step bringing her closer to Derrick and the future they were about to build together.

The aisle was lined with wildflowers, their bright colors a nod to the island they both adored. Chloe smiled, thinking how perfect it was that their wedding reflected the place that had brought them back together.

As she reached the altar, Derrick extended his hand. She took it, feeling the warmth and strength in his grip. His eyes were a brilliant green, filled with love and a hint of moisture. He squeezed her hand gently, a silent reassurance that this was where they were meant to be.

"Dearly beloved," began the pastor, but Chloe barely heard him. She was lost in Derrick's gaze, remembering the journey that had brought them here. The arguments, the misunderstandings, the reconciliations—it had all been worth it. She could almost see the same memories reflected in Derrick's eyes.

When it was time for their vows, Derrick went first. He spoke with a calm, steady voice, his words infused with the depth of his feelings. "Chloe, I've loved you from the moment you visited my table at Bravissimo. I know I've made mistakes, but they led me back to you and back to the Lord. I promise to cherish you, to honor you, and to love you every day for the rest of our lives. I promise to be your anchor in the storm, your lighthouse in the dark, and your partner along the way."

Chloe's eyes filled with tears. She took a deep breath, steadying herself before speaking. "Derrick, you came back into my life when I least expected it, but when I needed it the most. You've shown me that love can endure, that it can grow stronger even after being tested. I promise to stand by you, to support you, and to love you with all my heart."

As the pastor pronounced them husband and wife, Derrick leaned in and kissed her deeply, leaning her backward over his arm in a dramatic display of affection. The kiss was filled with promise and passion, an anticipation more than six years in the making. The applause of their friends and family washed over them, but Chloe was only aware of Derrick, his arms around her, his love enveloping her.

Outside, the sun was beginning to set, casting a golden glow over the island. They made their way to the reception, a simple but elegant affair held in a large tent on the beach.

The evening was filled with laughter and joy. Chloe danced with Derrick under the twinkling fairy lights, the sound of the waves a soothing backdrop. They shared their first meal as husband and wife, surrounded by nearly every resident of Sanctuary Island, along with a few friends from Chicago.

As the night wore on, they slipped away from the party, seeking a moment of solitude. They walked along the beach, the cool sand under their feet and the moonlight casting a silver path on the water. Chloe leaned into Derrick, feeling his strength and warmth.

"This is perfect," she murmured.

"You're perfect," Derrick responded, pulling her closer. "I've never been happier."

Chloe looked up at him, her heart full. "Definitely not perfect," she said, shaking her head.

"Perfect for me," he amended, his lips pressing against hers again.

She sighed after the kiss ended, laying her head on his chest as they stared into the dark water as the stars poked through the inky sky.

They stood there in silence for a while, soaking in the beauty of the moment.

"I love you," she whispered.

"I love you too," Derrick replied, kissing the top of her head.

"I'm so glad you came back. I can't imagine my life without you."

"Neither can I," Derrick said softly. "I'm just grateful

you gave me another chance. I'll never stop being grateful that God had a plan for the two of us."

"In His time," Chloe added, her lips tilting into a smile. Six years felt like forever, but she knew that it had been perfect timing.

♡♡♡

Return to Sanctuary Island in the next book in the series.

Our favorite sassy charter flight pilot, Angelica gets her story in Surrendering to Love by Kristen Fraser.

When love takes flight, redemption finds its harbor.

note to reader

Thank you for picking up (or downloading!) this book. If you enjoyed it, please consider taking a minute to leave a review or rating.

I loved writing Chloe and Derrick's story and helping them overcome their history and differences in opinion! Watching the line shift from enemies to frenemies to friends to love is so rewarding.

Be sure to check out the rest of the Love on Sanctuary Shores series, you can find them all on the next page.

If you loved Fighting for Her Heart and want to read more from me, check out The Bloom Sisters Series, starting with Hoping for Hawthorne. You'll visit Shaun's hometown of Minden, Indiana and discover a whole world of small-town romances.

I pray my books encourage you in your faith and

through your struggles, whatever they may be. I love hearing the amazing ways God has used my words in the lives of my readers. It is incredibly humbling and encouraging! You can email me anytime at taragraceericson@gmail.com.

You can also learn more about my upcoming projects at my website: www.taragraceericson.com or by signing up for my newsletter there. Just for signing up, you'll get two free ebooks and the audiobook of Hawthorne Bloom's story in Hoping for Hawthorne.

Thank you again for all your support and encouragement.

love on sanctuary shores

Welcome to the shores of Sanctuary Island, where six bestselling authors of Christian romance bring you stories of love and redemption. From tender romance to enduring faith, each standalone novel in this series promises unforgettable characters and heartwarming small town charm.

View the Series on Amazon

Tumbling into Tomorrow by Juliette Duncan (Harper and Nate)

Fighting for Her Heart by Tara Grace Ericson (Chloe and Derrick)

Surrendering to Love by Kristen M Fraser (Angie and Colton)

Running into Forever by Jennifer Rodewald (Sonora and Taylor)

Trusting His Promise by Valerie M Bodden (Josephine and Beckett)

Wishing for Mistletoe by Robin Lee Hatcher (Ariel and Tom)

acknowledgments

Above all – Thank You Lord, for giving me another story and the opportunity to sit at the table with the amazing women who created this series. I know I fail in so many ways, but your continued grace and provision is humbling.

To the authors of "Not Mackinac Island" aka Sanctuary Shores – Thank you for your dedication and heart for the Lord. You are all inspiring women of God. I'm honored to be included in this group.

Thanks to Elizabeth Maddrey and Jessica Barber for reading and giving me feedback on how to make this story and characters really shine.

To my copy editor – Brandi from Editing Done Write. Thank you for your encouragement and for fixing all my tenses and comma errors!

To my assistants - Missy, Carla, and Jenn. You ladies keep this ball rolling!

And finally, to my husband. You're my sanctuary. Thanks for indulging my bed-and-breakfast research trips and for the consistency with which you choose me and our family.

about the author

Tara Grace Ericson lives in Missouri with her husband and three sons. She studied engineering and worked as an engineer for many years before embracing her creative side to become a full-time author. Now, she spends her days chasing her boys and writing books when she can.

She loves cooking, crocheting, and reading books by the dozen. She loves a good "happily ever after" with an engaging love story. That's why Tara focuses on writing clean contemporary romance, with an emphasis on Christian faith and living. She wants to encourage her readers with stories of men and women who live out their faith in tough situations.

If you loved Fighting for Her Heart and want to read more from Tara, check out The Bloom Sisters Series, starting with Hoping for Hawthorne!

Printed in Great Britain
by Amazon

47882698R00179